WILD SWANS

JESSICA SPOTSWOOD

sourcebooks
fire

Published by Sourcebooks Fire, an imprint of Sourcebooks, Inc.
P.O. Box 4410, Naperville, Illinois 60567-4410
(630) 961-3900
Fax: (630) 961-2168
www.sourcebooks.com

Library of Congress Cataloging-in-Publication data is on file with the publisher.

Printed and bound in the United States of America.
VP 10 9 8 7 6 5 4 3 2 1

To all the girls with thirsty hearts
who worry that you aren't enough.
(you are.)
And for my mom, who is nothing like Erica.

WILD SWANS

by Edna St. Vincent Millay

I looked in my heart while the wild swans went over.
And what did I see I had not seen before?
Only a question less or a question more;
Nothing to match the flight of wild birds flying.
Tiresome heart, forever living and dying,
House without air, I leave you and lock your door.
Wild swans, come over the town, come over
The town again, trailing your legs and crying!

CHAPTER ONE

GRANDDAD SAYS ALL THE MILBOURN WOMEN ARE *EXTRAORDINARY*.

Amelia, the Shakespeare professor up at the college, says *cursed*.

Judy, the bookseller down at the Book Addict, says *crazy*.

Here in Cecil, girls are still expected to be *nice*. Quiet. All sugar. Maybe a little spice.

But not us. We Milbourn women are a complicated lot.

The Milbourn legacy goes back four generations. Folks were just starting to drive over from Baltimore and Washington, DC, to buy my great-great-grandmother's portraits when she tried outracing a train in her new roadster. It stalled on the tracks and she and her two youngest were killed instantly. My great-grandmother Dorothea survived and went on to win the Pulitzer Prize for her love poems—but she was murdered by the woman whose husband she'd been sleeping with for inspiration. Grandmother painted famous, haunting landscapes of the Bay, but the year before I was born, she walked out the back door and down to the water and drowned herself. My mother had a voice like a siren, but she ran away from home the second time she got knocked up, and we haven't seen her since.

And me? I don't feel crazy or cursed. But I've grown up in this house, haven't I? So I don't know. Maybe there's no escaping it.

I'm home alone tonight, and a storm is sweeping up the Bay. Through the open french doors I can hear the waves crashing against the shore. They make a frantic *shh-shh*, like a desperate mama rocking a colicky baby.

I hear mothers do things like that, anyhow. I wouldn't know.

I've been reading *Jane Eyre* for about the twelfth time, but I set it down on the coffee table and leave the warm lamplight to go stand in the doorway. The wind catches at my hair and flings it back in my face. I push it away and squint down at the beach.

Lightning hasn't split the sky yet, but I can taste it coming. The air's so thick I could swim through it.

Jesus, but a swim right now would be delicious. I imagine tearing off my blue sundress, running down the sandy path, and diving right into the cool waves of the Chesapeake. I could swim almost before I could walk. Part fish, Granddad says. But he doesn't like me to swim by myself. Says it isn't safe, especially for a girl, alone and at night. That's one of his rules. He's got about a million. Some of them I fight; some I just let be. Given how his wife killed herself, it seems reasonable enough to humor him on this.

Behind me, something rattles in the wind and I startle. Goose bumps prickle my shoulders in spite of the heat. Lately it feels like a storm's coming even when the sky's blue. Like spiders crawling through my veins.

My friend Abby tells me I need to quit worrying and relax. It's going to be golden, this summer before our senior year. There will be barbecues and bonfires and lazy days volunteering at the town library. She doesn't believe in family curses or premonitions of doom. Her family has its own troubles, but they're not town lore.

My friend Claire says "fuck the family curse; you're your own woman." Claire's all rebellion and razor-sharp edges—especially since her dad had an affair with his secretary and moved out (such a cliché). Claire doesn't believe in fate; she believes in making choices and owning them.

But she's not a Milbourn girl.

The rain starts with a fury. It pelts the windowpanes and drums against the flagstones out on the patio. The wind picks up too, sending the gray curtains spinning into the room like ghosts. I pad back toward the sofa, trailing my fingers across bookshelves stacked with Great-Grandmother Dorothea's prize-winning poetry. All along the walls hang Grandmother's landscapes—our pretty Eastern Shore transformed by twisting rain clouds. She only painted hurricane weather.

They were all so talented. Troubled, sure. But look at their legacy.

What will mine be?

Granddad's had me in all kinds of classes: piano, flute, ballet, gymnastics, oil painting, watercolors, landscapes, portraits, creative writing... I threw myself into every new subject, only to be crushed when I didn't show a natural aptitude for any of it.

I'm on the swim team, but I'm never going to be an Olympic athlete. I'm an honors student, but I won't be valedictorian. Sometimes I write poems, but that's just to get the restless thoughts out of my head; my poems have never won any awards. I am completely, utterly *ordinary*.

Granddad won't give up; he thinks there's some bit of genius hiding in me somewhere. But over the last couple months... Well, I'm getting tired of trying so hard only to end up a disappointment. Maybe that's not how this works. Maybe whatever spark blessed or cursed the other Milbourn girls skipped a generation.

To hear people in town talk, the women in my family

weren't just gifted; they were obsessed. And those obses-
sions killed them, three generations in a row. Maybe four.
For all I know, my mother could be dead now too. Do I
really want to continue that tradition?

Outside, thunder growls. Inside, something rattles. I
stare up at the portrait of Dorothea as it twitches against the
exposed brick wall. *Just the wind*, I reassure myself. *There's
no such thing as ghosts.*

Dorothea was fifteen when her mother painted her. She
wears a royal-blue shirtdress and matching gloves, and her
hair falls in short brown curls around her face. She wasn't
what you'd call pretty—too sharp featured for that—but
there's something captivating about her. She stands tall in
the portrait, shoulders back, lips quirked. It's not quite a
smile. More like a smirk. A year later, she'd survive the
collision that killed her mother and sisters. Her broken leg
never healed quite right, Granddad says; she walked with a
limp the rest of her life.

Lightning flashes. The lamp flickers. Rain is puddling on
the wooden floor. I should close the doors, but Dorothea's
eyes catch mine and somehow I don't want to turn my
back on her portrait.

There's no such thing as ghosts, I remind myself.

Then the room plunges into darkness.

I run for the french doors, but before I can get there, I
slam into something. Some*one*.

My heart stutter-stops and I shriek, scrambling away, slipping on the wet wooden floor.

"Ivy!" Alex grabs my arm. His fingers are warm against my skin. "It's just me. Chill."

"Jesus! I thought you were a ghost!" I take a deep breath, inhaling the salty breeze off the Bay. My pulse is racing.

"Nope, just me." He waves a flashlight. "Soon as the lights started flickering, Ma told me to bring you this. She knows how you get about the dark."

I fold my arms across my chest. "Shut up. I'm not scared of the dark anymore."

"Uh-huh. Sure." Alex shines the flashlight up over his face like a movie monster. I should have known better than to mention ghosts. He'll tease me about it forever. Remind me how he used to sneak over and scare Claire and me during sleepovers, how I used to sleep in my closet during thunderstorms, how I had a night-light till I turned thirteen.

"Gimme that." I reach for the flashlight.

"If you're not scared, why do you need it?" He holds it above his head. I'm tall—five ten—but the summer we were fourteen, Alex got taller, and he still hasn't stopped lording it over me. As he stretches, his shirt lifts to reveal taut, tanned abs.

I drag my eyes back to his face, but sort of leisurely like. He got soaked on his sprint from the carriage house, and his red T-shirt is molded to his muscled shoulders. The summer we were fifteen, he started lifting for baseball, and the girls at school went all swoony over him. I am not immune to a nice set of abs myself—but Alex is my best friend. Has been since we were babies, since my mother ran off and Granddad hired Alex's mom, Luisa, to be our housekeeper. There's nothing romantic between Alex and me.

That's what we decided after prom. What *I* decided. Alex and Luisa and Granddad are the only family I've got. What would happen if Alex and I started dating and it didn't work out? It would be awkward and awful, and I don't want to risk that. And if it did work? The baseball coach up at the college has already scouted Alex, all but promised him a scholarship if he keeps his grades up this year. If we were dating, Alex would be one more thing tying me to Cecil.

"I hate you," I mutter.

"No you don't." He gives me a cocky grin. Sometimes I think he's waiting for me to change my mind about us, but I'm not going to. Once I make a decision, I stick with it.

But the house presses around us, cold and quiet and more than a little spooky, and I fight the urge to snuggle up against him.

The front door slams. "Ivy!" Granddad hollers.

Just in time to save me from myself.

Alex relinquishes the flashlight. "I better go." Granddad

gets a little skittish about Alex being here when I'm home alone. Alex and I have never given him any reason not to trust us, but when your only daughter goes and gets herself pregnant twice before the age of twenty, you maybe have reason to be a little overprotective.

Like I said, I pick my battles.

"You going to be okay now that the Professor's home? No more ghosts?" Alex licks a raindrop from his upper lip and smiles. It's his placating-Ivy smile, the one that says I let my imagination run away with me. The one he uses when I get all dreamy over a boy in a book or want to watch an old black-and-white movie or point out shapes in the clouds. The one that makes me feel like maybe I am a Milbourn girl after all—sensitive and selfish and bound for a bad end.

I grit my teeth, but the worry in his brown eyes is genuine. "Yep. I'll be fine."

"Okay. See you." He jogs off through the rainy backyard.

"Ivy?" Granddad cusses as he knocks into something out in the hall.

"In here!" I pull the french doors shut.

He limps into the room, tossing his battered briefcase onto the sofa. He nods at me and the flashlight. "How long has the power been off?"

"Not long. Couple minutes." I smile as he heads right for Dorothea's crooked portrait and straightens it. He might be a professor, but he's only absentminded when he wants to be.

"What've you been up to?" he asks.

"Nothing. Reading." I wave my copy of *Jane Eyre* at him.

"Reading isn't nothing, young lady. Not in this house." He gives me a smile that doesn't quite reach his eyes and plops down into his brown leather recliner. "Have a seat. There's something I want to talk to you about."

That feeling slams into me again—impending doom—and I shiver. My skin feels like it's coated in cobwebs. "What's wrong?"

"Nothing we can't handle." Granddad stares up at Dorothea. "You know that student of mine? The one who's working in my office this summer?"

"Connor Clarke." As if I could forget. He's a rising sophomore who's somehow made himself indispensable. He aced Granddad's upper-level Twentieth Century American Poets course last semester.

Granddad nods. "I invited him over for lunch tomorrow. Remind me to leave a note for Luisa."

I raise my eyebrows. "Tomorrow's Wednesday."

He runs a hand over his bristly gray beard. "And?"

"Wednesday is Luisa's day off. Has been for years."

"Ah, I forgot." He steeples his fingers together. "You work the late shift tomorrow, don't you? Maybe you could join us."

Like I said—he's only forgetful when it suits him. "And make you lunch?"

He shrugs. "You might enjoy yourself. Connor's a good kid. Smart. Driven. He wrote an excellent paper on Dorothea. Most students are too intimidated to write a critical essay about my mother-in-law. It earned him an A on the paper *and* in the class."

"So you've mentioned." He hardly ever gives As in that class. Connor's probably an insufferable suck-up. "Impressive for a freshman."

"Would've been impressive for a senior." Granddad grins. He gets a kick out of my "competitive spirit," as he calls it. But he's the one who raised me to be ambitious, to think I could do anything I put my mind to. "I offer that class every spring. You could take it yourself."

We've had this conversation a million times. "*If* I stay here"—which I might, because I'd get free tuition and the college has a good swim team and a strong English program, and I worry about leaving Granddad all alone— "I'm not taking your classes. It would be too weird."

"It wouldn't be weird unless you made it weird," he insists. "You'd have to earn your B like everybody else."

"Except Connor," I grumble, bristling that he thinks this boy is smarter than me.

"Connor's an exceptional young man." Granddad casts a dubious look at *Jane Eyre*. "Really, Ivy. You'd rather study the nineteenth-century English novel than twentieth-century American poetry?"

I stick out my tongue at him. "I am *dying* to take Amelia's class on the nineteenth-century English novel, and you know it. Her Women in Shakespeare too."

Granddad sighs. "No accounting for taste, I suppose."

I grin, flopping back against the worn leather sofa. "You're the one who raised me to be a feminist. And you're perfectly capable of using the stove yourself, but I suppose I can make you and Connor some lunch. He's not a vegetarian, is he?"

"Oh, I hope not." Granddad shudders. "He seems so promising."

I smile, tucking my feet beneath me. "Is that all you wanted to talk about? The way you looked, I thought it was something dire."

"Actually…" He clears his throat. Drums his fingers on the armrest. The back of my neck prickles; it isn't like him to hem and haw. "I heard from your mother today."

"My—mother?" The word feels foreign on my tongue, like one you read in books and know how to spell but never learn to pronounce.

I must have misheard. Granddad hasn't talked to my mother in years. She signed away her rights to me when I was four, and he hasn't been in touch with her since.

Has he?

The lamp flickers back on. It illuminates the tired slump of his shoulders, the crow's feet perching next to his blue eyes. "Erica called me at the office. She… Well, the gist of it is that she's being evicted from her apartment and needs a place to stay. She asked to come home. I told her that I had to talk to you first, but I don't see how we can say no."

She left before I was two years old. Got pregnant again, dropped out of college, ran off with her boyfriend to New York City, and hasn't looked back since. Not once. Granddad says it's impossible for me to remember her, but I do. I think I do. White-blond hair and a smoky alto.

"*I* could say no." I click off the flashlight. "She needs a place to stay, so suddenly she remembers we exist? That's bullshit. That's not how family works."

I've never gotten a birthday card from her. Not a single Christmas present.

Granddad sighs, pinching the bridge of his long nose. Same nose as mine. What did I inherit from my mother? Her height? Her mouth? There are so few pictures from when she was my age.

Maybe she took them with her.

Or maybe she threw them away. Maybe she didn't want the memories any more than she wanted us.

When I was little, I prayed for her to come home.

But I'm seventeen now, and this is way too little, way too late.

"I know," Granddad says. He's the one who raised me to believe that family is everything: duty and love and legacy. "But we have to think about your sisters."

"*Sisters?*" I clutch the flashlight, knuckles white. "More than one?"

"Came as a surprise to me too. Isobel is fifteen. Grace"— his voice wobbles. That was Grandmother's name—"is six."

I've got sisters. Two of them. I wonder if they are perfect little Milbourn girls with marvelous talents. I wonder if they know that I exist.

"I know this won't be easy for you, Ivy. It won't be easy for me either. But Erica and her husband are getting divorced, and she lost her job, and she needs a place to stay. It took a lot for her to ask. I couldn't turn her away." He avoids my eyes and fiddles with his big, silver watch.

Those are his tells. Granddad is a terrible poker player.

"You already said yes," I realize. "When are they coming?"

"Saturday."

That's four days from now. I run my fingers through my long hair, catching at the tangles. "I see." My voice is frosty.

"It's only temporary. Just till she can earn some money and get back on her feet. I'm sure she'll want to get the girls back to their schools in September."

"September? But that's the whole summer!"

And this summer was supposed to be *perfect*.

Every summer, Granddad signs me up for activities:

writing camp up at the college or watercolors at the Arts League or a production of *Oklahoma* at the Sutton Theater. This year I put my foot down: no,classes. I'm volunteering at the library and I'll be swimming every day. I *need* this, I told Granddad—a real summer. A break before senior year and all its pressures: captaining the swim team, copyediting the yearbook, taking three AP classes, and applying for college. And most of all (though I didn't say this part) I am desperate for a break from the restless, relentless search for my talent.

Granddad agreed, as long as I promised to submit some of my poems for publication.

How am I supposed to relax with my mother and newfound sisters living here all summer long.

"Can she do that?" I ask. "Take them out of New York? Their dad won't mind?"

"I don't get the sense that Isobel has a relationship with her father, and Grace's dad—" Granddad clears his throat, avoiding my gaze again. "They don't live in New York. Haven't for a while. They're over in DC now."

"Oh. I see," I say again.

And I do. Clear as day. My mother's been living two hours away, and she still couldn't be bothered to come visit. To join us for Thanksgiving dinner. To cheer me on at one of my swim meets.

I'm not even worth a tank of gas.

BONG. BONG. BONG.

The doorbell gives another stately chime, and I give the table one last glance. I've set it with our blue-flowered china and plunked a vase of daisies in the middle. With rain pattering on the windows and a loaf of French bread baking in the oven, the kitchen is downright homey.

I might be a mess, but there's no reason perfect Connor Clarke needs to know that.

Bong. Bong. Bong.

"Ivy, can you get that?" Granddad hollers from his office.

He's on the phone with Erica. They've been talking for a while now, his voice rising and falling like choppy waves against the dock. They're already fighting.

Maybe he'll tell her she can't come.

"Got it!" I hurry down the hall, past the living room we hardly ever use, pausing to tighten the knot on my halter dress. I put it on this morning because the cherry print is cute and I thought it might cheer me up some, but it's a little lower cut than I remembered. Last thing I need to do is go flashing Granddad's pet student.

I hardly slept last night. My mother is going to be here in three days—my mother and the sisters I've never met. I've been texting Abby and Claire all morning, but I still can't wrap my mind around it.

I take a deep breath, plaster on a smile, and throw open the front door. A guy is standing on our porch, staring out at the rain. Beyond him, the sky is gray and gloomy. This weather feels portentous—a day for omens, for strange birds and black dogs and bells tolling thirteen times.

Abby would tell me I sound like Catherine Morland, the silly, gothic novel–obsessed heroine of *Northanger Abbey*. Claire would tell me to stop being so dramatic and check out the guy in front of me, and Claire would be right, because *wow*.

I was expecting Connor Clarke to be tall and lanky as a green bean, with hipster glasses and floppy hair. He'd wear skinny jeans and Chucks and a *Doctor Who* T-shirt. That's the type of boy who usually takes Granddad's poetry classes.

The boy on the porch is tall—he looms over me—but that's about all I got right.

I notice his ink first. Tattoos creep like morning glory vines over his arms, then disappear beneath the sleeves of his black T-shirt. He's not white; that was a stupid assumption. He's biracial, maybe, or Mexican American like Alex, with smooth, light-brown skin and black hair cropped close to his head.

I catch myself staring. "Um, hey. You must be Connor."

He turns. "You must be Ivy. Nice to meet you." He sticks out a hand for me to shake. His fingers are splattered with ink. Not the permanent kind, but as though he's been writing with a fountain pen. His eyes are a rich golden brown, and they skewer me like a worm on a hook. "I've heard a lot about you."

"You too." I duck my chin, suddenly shy. Granddad's had me shaking hands since I was a toddler, but it's different when the guy is cute, and Connor Clarke is beyond cute. He isn't classically handsome; his jaw is too square, his nose broad but crooked, like it was broken once, and his ears stick out a little. But he's interesting looking, and the tattoos... I never thought I found tattoos hot, but apparently I do. On him I do.

I clear my throat. "Come on in. Granddad'll be down in a second."

"Thanks." He steps inside and lets out a low whistle.

"Professor said this place has been in the Milbourn family for generations. All the way back to Dorothea's mother."

"Yep." I watch as Connor examines the framed photos of Dorothea. There she is on her wedding day; there she is accepting her Pulitzer; there she is getting an honorary doctorate from the college. I complained to Granddad once that there aren't more pictures of him and me around the house, and he said just as soon as I get my PhD or my Pulitzer, he'll put my photo up right next to hers.

Thanks for setting the bar so low, Dorothea.

"I'm a huge fan of her work. This is so cool," Connor says, a reverent note in his voice, and this big, dorky grin spreads over his face.

I nod, because what am I supposed to say? That sometimes I feel like I'm growing up in a museum, a shrine to our family's history of mental illness? That Dorothea's poetry was beautiful, but she destroyed two families because she flaunted her affair all over town? She was shot and killed, her lover was paralyzed from the waist down, and his wife was sent to prison. Four children—Grandmother and the three Moudowney kids—grew up without mothers. I find it hard to feel reverent about someone responsible for that.

Obviously Connor feels differently. So does Granddad.

"Did you grow up here?" Connor asks.

"Yep." I hope he won't ask about my parents.

Or maybe he already knows about my mother. Erica

called Granddad at the office; maybe Connor's the one who answered the phone. It's strange to think he might have talked to her. I wonder if she sounds like I remember, if my memory of swaying around in her arms is real or just a story someone told me once.

Has she ever looked me up online? I searched for her last night. Couldn't find much. No Facebook profile.

It would help if I knew her last name.

I wonder if my sisters are Milbourn girls. Grandmother kept the Milbourn name when she and Granddad got married, then passed it on to my mother, who—maybe on account of not knowing who my father was—gave it to me.

I glance up, realizing I've been quiet too long and Connor's waiting for me to say something. *Jesus, Ivy, get it together.* "What about you? Where are you from?"

"DC." He smells like coffee. I wonder if he was scribbling poems with his fountain pen in a coffee shop. "Near H Street," he adds.

I shrug an apology. "I'm not real familiar with DC."

But Erica and my sisters live there. For all I know, they could be Connor's neighbors.

"It's a cool neighborhood. Lot of gentrification over the last couple years though. Folks like my gram get pushed out to make way for hipsters." He shakes his head. "Don't get me started."

I smile and smooth the red hem of my skirt. "Can I get you something to drink? Iced tea?"

His eyes land on my legs and I catch him looking. "Uh, no. No thanks."

I can't believe this guy is Granddad's suck-up student. He's six feet three at least, with ripped arms and broad shoulders that taper to a narrow waist. He looks like a goddamn quarterback. As he scrubs a hand over his head, the words tattooed on his right bicep snag my attention; they're as familiar as breathing. "Is that from Dorothea's 'Second Kiss'?"

He grins, pushing up his sleeve so I can get a better glimpse of the poem that curves over his skin. "Yeah. It's one of my favorites." He flips his arm over, revealing lines from another poem spiraling like a snail across his forearm. "I've got Langston Hughes here. And Edna St. Vincent Millay here." He taps his chest.

"I love Millay." I wonder which poem it is, what it means to him. Why he chose to have it inscribed right over his heart.

Hell, now I'm picturing him without his shirt on, all muscles and poetry and—

I stare down at my bare feet, flushing.

"The Professor said you're a poet too." Connor shares it casually, but my head snaps up, my body tensing like a bowstring.

"What? No." I bite my lip. "That's not true."

"Oh." Connor squints at me. "Sorry, I must have misunderstood."

But he didn't. I know he didn't, and I *hate* it when Granddad goes around talking me up, making it sound like I'm special when I'm not. "No. He probably did say that. He exaggerates. I write a little. Sometimes. It's not really my thing."

"Right." Connor's lips twitch. "So what is your thing?"

My shoulders hunch. "I don't have one. Not everybody has a thing."

Connor does though. It's tattooed all over him.

I'm being kind of weird and prickly, but he plows ahead, unheeding. "Your family's full of such incredible artists I guess I just assumed that—"

"You know what they say about assuming." I'm trying to tease, but it comes out more of a rebuke. I shrug. "I'm not like the rest of my family. I'm ordinary."

And now I sound *pathetic.* I fold my arms over my chest. Connor's gaze dips down to my cleavage, and I fight against a blush when, a second later, his eyes meet mine.

"Nope," he says. "I don't believe that."

Hold up. Is he flirting with me?

Jesus, his eyes are pretty. They've got little gold flecks near the center.

I glance down to collect my composure, and when I look up, he's examining Dorothea's pictures again.

I'm so stupid. Connor isn't interested in me; he's interested in the Milbourn legacy. He wrote a whole paper on my great-grandmother.

It stings more than it should.

"You don't know anything about me. You have no idea what it means to be a Milbourn," I say.

"So tell me," Connor says, and for a minute I am tempted to do just that. Spill all my messy secrets.

"Ivy? Connor?" Granddad's loafers squeak against the floor outside his office, and then his footsteps pad down the stairs. "There you are. Good to see you, Connor."

"Hey, Professor. You've got a beautiful house."

"Thank you." Granddad's voice sounds like a thread about to snap. I want to ask him how the phone call went, what Erica said—but not in front of Connor. "Ivy, the timer's going off in the kitchen. I could hear it through the vent. Is that lunch?"

"Oh *shit*. The bread!" I can't even make lunch right.

"Language, Ivy," Granddad chides.

"Sorry." I run for the kitchen.

They follow me. "It's our housekeeper's day off, so Ivy made us lunch," Granddad says.

"Thanks, Ivy," Connor says, but I wince. Here I am whining about my family history, and he probably sees a privileged white girl who doesn't realize how lucky she has it. He wouldn't be wrong. I've grown up with every advantage. My college applications are going to be amazing.

But I'd trade every one of those private lessons for a normal family.

"You should come over for supper sometime when Luisa's here. Her spaghetti and meatballs are not to be missed," Granddad brags.

Connor smiles. "That sounds amazing. I miss my mother's cooking."

"Luisa's like a mother to me," I say, and immediately wish I could shove those defensive words back down my throat. It's true, but I don't owe Connor any explanations. Why am I letting him get me all rattled?

Connor nods politely, his face inscrutable.

Great. Now he must think I'm crazy. Or awful enough that I have to pay someone to act like my mother.

· · · · ·

Lunch is awkward. Granddad and Connor talk about poetry while I stare out the window at the choppy, gray waves beating against the shore. I think about my mother. Wonder what she's really like. I've heard stories—not from Granddad, who seldom speaks of her, but from Amelia when she comes over for faculty parties and has a second glass of pinot grigio.

People in Cecil love to gossip about my family. I've grown up with old ladies calling me a poor dear and then whispering behind my back. They talk about how *troubled* my mother was, or they say she was a real handful, that she drank too much and slept around and put the poor Professor through the wringer.

Then there's my grandmother. Some people say it was a real shame what happened to Grace. Some say she was selfish to leave her daughter and husband. Others say it was fate—that the Milbourn women are all reckless and bound for bad ends. Dorothea went and had that affair and got herself murdered, didn't she? And her mother... Well, Charlotte Milbourn didn't intend for any of her children to escape that train. Dorothea started keeping a journal soon afterward, a practice she kept till the day she died. She wrote plainly about everything else—plainly enough to make me blush sometimes—but not about the collision that took her mother and sisters' lives. That, she referred to just once. As "the accident." They never proved it was purposeful.

Cursed. Doomed. Crazy. The words are a drumbeat in the back of my mind. Once I found an old videotape of my mother singing in her middle school chorus. She was tall and blond and coltish, not grown into her arms and legs yet, gawky as hell. Amelia told me Erica was in a band later. Does she still sing, or did she run away from that too?

"Ivy?" Judging from the way he and Connor are

staring at me, expectant, it's not the first time Granddad has called my name. I drag my attention back to their conversation. "I was saying that you should show Connor your work sometime."

"My work?" I choke.

"Your poems. The ones you're planning to submit," he clarifies. Thank God he doesn't ask me to go get them. This brings back mortifying memories of command flute performances of "Silent Night" at the English department Christmas parties. "Connor's a talented poet."

"Of course he is." I stab at a piece of avocado. Why doesn't Granddad adopt Connor then?

Connor looks back and forth between Granddad, who's pageant-momming all over the place, and me, slumping sullenly in my chair. He stands. "I've got to get back to work. I'm doing a double at Java Jim's. But thanks for having me over, Professor. This was great. Thanks for making lunch, Ivy."

"You're welcome. It was nice to meet you," I mumble.

While Granddad walks him out, I clear the table. Without being asked. Like a good granddaughter. But I bang the plates a little. I would rather die than share my scribblings with Connor. Poetry is obviously his thing, and there's no doubt in my mind he's really good at it. I mean, he loves it enough to work in Granddad's office this summer. Enough to come over and have lunch with his professor and the professor's grumpy granddaughter. The way Connor talked about poetry—leaning forward in his chair, his ink-stained hands waving to illustrate his point, that big, goofy grin on his face—was dorky as hell but also kind of hot.

I wish I felt that way about something. *Consumed* by it.

My eyes fall on one of Grandmother's paintings. In it, the black sky twists and the waves rage.

I shiver. Maybe it's easier being ordinary.

Granddad pokes his head back into the kitchen. "You all right, Ivy Bear? You were awfully quiet at lunch."

"Fine," I mutter, sliding the clean cutting board onto the drying rack.

"You sure?" he presses. "I thought Connor made some good points about Emily Dickinson, but I can't imagine you agreed."

I dry my hands on the green dish towel. "Didn't think there was any point in arguing. He thinks awfully well of himself, doesn't he?"

As soon as I say it, I want to reel the bratty words back in.

Granddad braces his hands, ropy and twisted from arthritis, against one of the wooden chairs. "He's one of the brightest young men I've taught. I don't find him arrogant."

I sigh. "Neither do I. Not really. He was nice. I like his tattoos."

Granddad peers at me. "You look like somebody ran over your dog."

"You never let me have a dog." Too afraid it'd pee on Dorothea's carpets and chew on her books. Another price of living in the family museum.

"You know what I mean. You look upset."

"You sounded upset." I toss the towel onto the counter. "On the phone. What were you and Erica fighting about?"

"Nothing," Granddad says. "Just trying to figure out the details for the move. We'll get it all straightened out by Saturday."

He doesn't meet my eyes.

"Was it about me?" Asking is pressing on a bruise.

"What? No. Of course not. Your mother… Erica's not an easy person," he admits.

"Is she awful?" I ask.

Granddad hesitates. "She can be," he says. "She's stubborn. Lashes out and doesn't like to admit when she's wrong. Gets that from me, I guess." He tries a smile, but it falters. "We've always been like oil and water. Her mother knew how to manage her. They were pretty close. When Grace died, Erica was devastated. I couldn't… I didn't know how…"

He stares at the tiled floor. "I didn't know how to help her," he finishes. "I thought—hoped—that having you would turn things around. That she'd step up to the responsibility. But she didn't. And that's not on you, Ivy. There was something broken in her, and she had to want to fix it."

"Maybe she's different now," I say.

"Maybe." But he doesn't sound convinced. Whatever she said on the phone, it has him second-guessing his decision to let her come home.

I wish he'd tell her to stay away. We don't need her anymore. The days when I wished on every shooting star and birthday candle for my mama are long past, and now I don't want her here any more than she ever wanted me.

CHAPTER THREE

My mother was pretty.

As a little girl, she had white-blond hair and chubby, pink cheeks and big, brown eyes. She wore neon dresses and leg warmers and pink jelly shoes as she posed on the brick sidewalk downtown. In one photo, she holds Granddad's hand and a chocolate ice cream cone. In the next, Grandmother pushes her on the tire swing in the backyard.

As she gets older, there are fewer pictures. Teenage Erica is thin as a rail, swallowed up by plaid shirts and baggy jeans. I can tell by her dark roots and eyebrows that her spiky blond hair comes from a bottle. Her smiles are thorny and reluctant. There are hardly any photos of the whole family, just one at the English department Christmas party. Erica's skinny arms poke out of a velvety black dress. Granddad looks mostly the same, still tall and bearded, just thinner and less gray. Grandmother wears a purple dress and pearls, her brown hair tumbling down around her shoulders. She and Granddad stand close but not touching in a way that seems purposeful.

You could write it off as a bad night, a moody teenage girl and an argument, if you didn't know what was coming.

Six months later, my grandmother was dead, and a few months after that, Erica got pregnant with me. It was a one-night stand; she didn't even know my father's last name. I was an accident. A mistake she was glad to leave behind.

I wonder if she's dreading today as much as I am.

"Ivy?" Footsteps clomp up the attic stairs, and Alex's head pokes into my room. "Hey. Professor said I could come up."

"Hey." I'm sitting cross-legged on my bed, sweat soaked and anxious. Still wearing the red tank top and plaid shorts I slept in, my hair straggling out of yesterday's braid. I haven't been downstairs yet except to grab a blueberry muffin and the photo album. Granddad must be pretty worried if he's sending Alex up to my bedroom.

"I don't know how you breathe in here," Alex complains.

A fan whirs lazily in the corner, but it's still about a billion degrees. "I'm used to it."

He makes a face. "Ma said you didn't come down for lunch."

"Not hungry." Which isn't like me. *Ivy's healthy as a horse*, Granddad likes to say. He cannot abide girls who pick at their food.

Alex plops down on the bed next to me. "Ivy, you look like shit."

"Gee, thanks." We haven't talked for a couple days—not since the thunderstorm. I've been kind of hiding out. "My mother's coming today."

"I heard." He frowns. "I'd ask if you're okay, but…"

I'm fine, I want to say. But I can't make the lie come out of my mouth. Not to Alex. He's had a front-row seat to all my hurts and heartaches over the last fifteen years. He can tell when I'm lying.

I pick up the photo album and flip a couple pages. "This is what I looked like the last time she saw me."

Alex glances down at the picture. It's me as a toddler wearing a pair of jeans and a fuzzy orange sweater with a pumpkin on it. My brown curls are pulled into tiny pigtails, and I sit in Mama's lap while she reads me *The Poky Little Puppy*. In the picture, she's smiling down at me. A month later she was gone.

"You were real cute." Alex pokes me. "Still are." I don't smile, and he puts a hand on my arm. "Screw her, Ivy."

"I know." Claire's been texting me the same thing since

she found out, except she doesn't say "screw." *You don't owe that woman a fucking thing. She left you.* Forgiveness isn't really in Claire's skill set. Since her dad walked out on her mom, Claire has refused to see him. He bought her a car when she turned eighteen, and she sent it back to the dealership. Abby, on the other hand, is the optimist. The peacemaker. *Try to keep an open mind. Maybe she'll surprise you.*

I throw myself backward, stretching out on the rumpled blue quilt. It's easier to talk about my feelings without Alex looking at me. "I want her to hug me and say how sorry she is for leaving. That it wasn't my fault. But if she were that kind of person, that kind of *mother*—"

"She wouldn't have left in the first place."

"Yep." I sit up again and close the album with a crack. "I'm so mad at her. For leaving. For never once getting in touch. But what am I supposed to do? I can't change what happened. I've just got to suck it up and make the best of things."

"Do you? Seems to me she's the one ought to be walking on eggshells to make things easier on you, not the other way around."

"From what Granddad says, she's not the type to walk on eggshells. More like smash them." I let out a frustrated sigh. "It's so pathetic! I just want her to like me! Since when do I care so much about what people think?"

Alex runs a hand through his dark curls and laughs. "Since always?" He shakes his head. "She's not some random person. She's your mom. Of course you want her to like you. I just think you need to, like, manage your expectations."

"So I shouldn't have booked that mother-daughter spa day?" I raise my eyebrows. "Trust me, my expectations are set low. Way low. I mean, she never even sent me a birthday card." My voice drops to a whisper, and I cover my face with my hand. "What did I do to make her hate me so much?"

Alex yanks on my elbow, hauling my hand away from my face. Traitorous tears are gathering in my eyes. "You didn't do anything. You were just a baby. Whatever her deal is, it's with the Professor, not you. You know how he can be."

I pull away. I do know how he can be. The weight of his expectations is heavy, but that is no excuse for running out on your family. "Don't you make excuses for her. Granddad—he's a good person. A good father."

Alex puts his hands up. "Hey, you don't have to convince me. He's the closest thing I've ever had to a dad."

Alex's father died in a car accident a few weeks before Erica left town. Marco and Luisa had just moved from Texas. Marco had gotten a job as an associate professor of math at the college. Once he got tenure and Alex got old enough for preschool, Luisa was going to open up her own bakery. Instead, her husband died, she became our house-keeper, and she and Alex moved into the carriage house. They've been there ever since.

I can't imagine how lonely life would be without them.

"I'm just saying, the Professor can be a little intense." Alex stands and stretches, cracking his neck in the way that always makes me cringe. "Hey, when's the last time you went for a swim?"

"I don't know. It's been raining all week. Tuesday?"

"No wonder you're in a mood." He grabs a slim collection of Langston Hughes poetry from my nightstand and fans himself with it. I may or may not have been looking up Connor's tattoos. "Your gills are gonna grow shut."

"My gills?" I laugh despite myself.

"Professor always says you're part fish. Come on. What's that saying? Nothing salt water can't cure? Besides, we stay up here much longer, I'm gonna melt."

I check my phone. "They'll be here in an hour."

"Still time for a swim. Come on. Race me 'cross the channel and back?" Alex winks. "I'll let you win."

I jump up. "The hell you will."

He's already on the steps. "That a yes?"

"When was the last time you beat me?" I rummage through my dresser for my swimsuit.

He pokes his nose between the slats in the railing.

"Last week at Scrabble. And week before that, I beat you and Ma and the Professor at croquet."

"Scrabble was only 'cause you cheated and looked up *Z* words on your phone," I remind him. "That doesn't count. And I meant swimming."

"It's been a while. I feel like today's the day though. Seeing how you're all sad and shit. Might make you slow." He grins at me. I've never been able to back down from a challenge, especially one issued with Alex's cocky smile. That's how I sprained my ankle jumping off the sunroom roof into a snowdrift when we were ten.

Mostly it turns out okay though.

"Get out of here so I can change." I grab a pillow and throw it at him. It misses because I have terrible aim, and he laughs and clatters down the stairs. That boy knows me too damn well.

Right now I'm grateful for it.

I change into my swimsuit: a red one-piece with skinny straps and high-cut legs. It's retro cute but sturdy. Claire and Abby keep telling me I ought to buy a bikini. Claire's got a black one that makes just about every boy in town drool, and Abby's got one with a pink-and-green bandeau top that's so barely there I get nervous for her every time she jumps off the dock. And she's got a lot less up top than I do. Anyway, I keep telling them there is no point in having a swimsuit that I can't actually swim in.

I'm not fat. But it's hard to remember that when I stand next to my friends. Claire's tall like me, but she's got that classic hourglass figure—big boobs, tiny waist, curvy hips. And Abby's five foot nothing and petite, the kind of girl that boys scoop up and toss in the pool. I'm—solid. With strong shoulders and thighs from swimming.

My phone chimes with a text. Speaking of Abby...

bonfire tonight. can you come?

maybe, I text back.

you deserve a party! summer of fun, remember?!

Right. **i'll try**

lmk how it goes with your mom

I glance in the mirror, straightening my freckled, muscled shoulders.

Erica and my sisters are coming whether I like it or not. No matter what happens this afternoon, it's not going to magically make up for fifteen years without them in my life. There's no point in staying up here being all sulky and sad, wasting good sunshine.

· · · · ·

It's pure gorgeous out: a true-blue sky with white cotton-ball clouds and the sun sparkling on the water like diamonds. Why didn't Grandmother paint the Bay like *this*?

As soon I'm in the water, I push all thoughts of mothers and sisters and family curses out of my head. I beat Alex back to the dock by a good three lengths. Alex is first baseman on the varsity baseball team and he'll probably get that scholarship, but he doesn't swim laps up at the college pool seven days a week like I usually do. I tell him next time I'll swim butterfly—my weakest stroke—to give him a fighting chance. He hooks a leg around my ankle and dunks me.

I come up laughing.

"Feel better?" he asks. I nod, and the way he looks at me feels like it did at prom. Like we could be more than just friends if I let us. If I wanted that.

My eyes linger on his mouth. What would it be like to kiss Alex?

Doesn't matter. I'm not willing to risk our friendship to find out.

I splash him instead. "What're you doing tonight? Abby said there's a bonfire. Wanna go?" Abby's been waitressing down at the Crab Claw the last two summers. The parties at the cove nearby are legendary, a boozy mix of townies and college kids.

Alex nods. "Couple guys from the team are going. You think the Professor will let you out?"

It took some convincing for Granddad to let me go out last summer, but I kept coming home in one piece without smelling like a keg, so I think I've earned his trust. "If you walk me and I promise to be responsible."

Alex rolls his eyes. "You're always responsible."

I flip onto my back and float. He's right. I'm pretty well behaved, generally. A couple kisses here and there, but nothing serious. Nobody I've wanted to get serious with. It helps that I hate the taste of beer and am therefore less tempted to do stupid, impulsive things. Sometimes I'll have a cup of cheap, fruity wine, but I never let myself get more than a little buzzed.

Probably has something to do with being conceived when Erica—a high school senior at the time—hooked up with a college boy at a frat party. She was messed up and mourning, and I try not to judge her for it, but some days I'm more successful than others. I've grown up without a mother, without even knowing my father's name. I'm not about to repeat Erica's mistakes.

"Ivy!" Luisa is walking down the sandy path. "Honey, they'll be here any minute."

I flip upright. My stomach tips and tumbles, and I want to dive under the water and stay there forever.

Instead I paddle over to the sun-warped wooden dock and hoist myself up. Grab the gray towel with the college's mascot—a crane, of all ridiculous things—and wrap it around my waist. Wring out my long hair.

"Want me to come with you?" Alex asks.

"Alex, I don't think—" Luisa's kind brown eyes, so like

his, dart back and forth between us. "I think it should just be family."

But Alex and Luisa *are* my family.

I fight the urge to take Alex's hand. I don't want to give him mixed signals. Right now I just want my friend, not this new—*whatever*—between us.

Only it's starting to feel like I can't get one without the other anymore.

Alex opens his mouth to argue, but I force a smile. "It's okay. I'll see you later."

I walk up the path and through the backyard, bare feet squelching in grass that's still soggy from last night's rain. I leave footprints on the gray floorboards as I creep around the porch. A car roars up the driveway. I should've gone inside sooner. Changed into something pretty. Now I'm going to meet them in a swimsuit and towel, with dripping hair and bare feet.

The car engine cuts out and doors slam. One, two, and—after a long pause—three.

No one blows a whistle, but I feel like it's time to dive into the deep end.

I'm about to step around the corner when I hear a voice. *Her* voice. I don't catch the words, just the gravel and honey mix of it, scratchy and slow. I *know* that voice. It fixes me in place. It's been fifteen years, but a tiny part of me still wants to run to her for a hug and a song. *Mama.*

I steady myself against the house, pulling strength from the warm, white bricks. My heart is racing as I poke my head out.

She doesn't look like somebody's mom.

That's my first, maybe uncharitable, thought. Abby's mom is a part-time real estate agent who wears capris and pastel T-shirts from the Gap. Claire's mom is a history professor who wears a lot of belted fifties-style shirtdresses. Erica is wearing black shorts so short they'd get her sent home from school and a black tank top that show off her long, skinny limbs. Her bleached-blond hair is swept to one side in a chic pixie cut. She's carrying a huge iced coffee in one hand and a cigarette in the other, and her eyes are hidden behind enormous sunglasses. She's tall—taller than me, I think, till I see the strappy gladiator sandals that give her a couple extra inches.

The front door bangs and Granddad's loafers slap across the porch, then the driveway. "Erica. It's good to see you." He goes to hug her and she takes a step back. *Ouch.*

"Dad." She gives a curt nod. "This is Grace." Grace is tall and skinny for six, with all of Erica's sharp angles. "And this is Isobel." Isobel is short and curvy, with a heart-shaped face that makes her look younger than fifteen. She and Grace have the same white-blond hair that Erica had when she was a little girl, which apparently skipped me.

The three of them stand together in a little triangle. A team. A *family*.

Loneliness knifes through me.

Stupid. So stupid. These people are strangers. Why do I care how they stand?

Granddad shoves his hands in the pockets of his khaki shorts. "Well, it's real nice to meet you girls."

"You're our grandpa, huh? Is that what I call you?" Grace pulls off her pink, star-shaped sunglasses and gazes up at him. "I never had a grandpa before. Daddy's daddy died before I was born."

"You could try Granddad. See how that feels," he suggests. "Or you could call me George."

"George!" Grace laughs. "Like Curious George?"

I can hear the smile creep into his voice. "Yep."

"You can call me Gracie. Everybody does, 'cept Mama," Grace says. "Oh, Mama, look! A porch swing! I *love* porch swings." She bounds past Granddad up to the porch, and I dart back before she can see me. "I think I'm going to like it here!" she announces.

"Mmm-hmm," Erica says, noncommittal, and I peek out in time to see her take a long drag from her cigarette. Gross.

Isobel looks around at the gabled old farmhouse and the fields that stretch out as far as the eye can see. "That makes *one* of us who wants to be here," she mutters, loud enough that I can hear. I know Cecil must be real different from what they're used to in New York and Washington, DC, but that's no excuse to be rude.

Enough. I can't let Granddad stand out there by himself.

"Hi." I'm proud that my voice doesn't shake or squeak.

Granddad turns. "There's our Ivy."

I resist the urge to hide behind him. I step up next to him instead and square my shoulders. Even with her crazy heels, I'm Erica's height. My eyes meet her mirrored sunglasses and I wonder what she's thinking. Am I how she pictured me?

She takes another drag of her cigarette and stares long enough that I want to squirm. "Jesus, you're tall."

I wait for her to say more.

She doesn't.

My mother hasn't seen me in fifteen years, and that's all she has to say to me?

"Five ten," I mumble, fighting the urge to slouch.

"I'm tall too," Gracie calls from the porch swing. "I'm going to be practically a giant. Like my daddy. He's six feet two inches tall." She scrutinizes me. "So you're my aunt Ivy, huh? I never had an aunt before. Just uncles."

My stomach drops like a stone.

"Your—" I choke, turning back to my mother. "*Aunt* Ivy?"

Erica pushes her sunglasses to the top of her head. Her big, brown eyes are rimmed in black and framed by long lashes. Fake, probably.

She stares at Granddad. "You didn't talk to her about this?"

"No. I thought we decided—" Granddad's voice is a teakettle just about to boil.

"No, *you* decided." She purses her lips. "I never agreed to anything."

CHAPTER FOUR

THE PAVEMENT IS HOT BENEATH MY BARE FEET AND THE SUN IS scorching the crown of my head, but I go icy with rage. This is what she and Granddad were arguing about on the phone. It has to be.

Granddad looks over his shoulder at Gracie. "This isn't… We'll talk about this once we get the girls settled."

Erica shrugs. "It's not up for debate. I told you that."

Why is she doing this? To hurt me? To prove that I'm nothing to her? The way she stands, head thrust forward, it's obvious that she's spoiling for a fight.

But not, I realize, with me. Her gaze never leaves Granddad. Alex was right; her problem is with him. She doesn't care about me or my feelings at all.

Hurt slices through me, like the time last summer I stepped on a shell and Alex had to carry me back to the house.

If Erica cared about me, she wouldn't have run off. Or she would have stayed in touch. Christmas cards. Birthday presents. Emails. Visits. *Something.* I don't know why I'm surprised.

I guess I'd hoped that maybe, deep down, she still felt something. A little bit of curiosity or interest or regret or—

Love.

Stupid. My mother doesn't love me. She never has.

My throat aches. Tears well up, and I blink them back. I will not cry in front of her.

Behind us, Gracie jumps off the porch swing with a thud. "Don't fight already, Mama," she pleads, all blond bounce and sparkle. "We just got here!"

I glance at Isobel. She's texting furiously on her blinged-out phone like she's not paying any attention to our argument. But her body language, tense and hunched, gives her away.

Gracie peers up at me. She's standing so close I can smell her strawberry bubble gum. "I thought you'd have yellow hair like Mama and Iz and me," she says.

I finger a wet brown curl. "Nope."

"Were you swimming?" she asks.

I wonder how often she does this. Jumps in and smooths things over for her mother. A six-year-old shouldn't have to do that. My frostbitten tongue thaws.

"Yep." I rewrap the gray towel around my waist. I've spent half my life in bathing suits. I know I look okay—not model skinny, but swimmer strong. Next to Erica though, I feel like a goddamn Amazon. "You like to swim?"

Gracie pouts. "I don't know how."

I gawk at her. I can't imagine a life without waves and weightlessness.

Gracie thaws Granddad too. "Well, we'll fix that," he declares. "Ivy'll teach you. She's going to be captain of her school's swim team next year. She came in second at regionals in the one-hundred-meter backstroke."

"No!" Erica's voice is louder than it needs to be. Loud enough that we all turn and stare. She throws her cigarette to the pavement. "I don't want you in the water, Grace."

"But, Mama!" Gracie whines.

"I said *no*!" Erica snaps, and Gracie wilts like week-old lettuce.

Granddad rubs a hand over his beard. "Erica, she can't spend the summer here without learning to swim. Don't be—"

"Don't you dare say 'ridiculous.' Considering what happened, what Mom—" Erica breaks off and her gaze darts past us, past the house to the glittering blue Bay, and for a second I think maybe she *does* have a heart. Coming back here after so long, back to the place where her mother drowned, can't be easy. I feel the tiniest pinprick of sympathy.

Doesn't last long.

"Of course not. I didn't mean…" Granddad says. "But the Bay's in our backyard. It's not safe for—"

"I said no, and I'm her mother." Erica stalks close, gets up in his face. "I make the decisions for my kids. Or else we're leaving right now."

"And going where?" Granddad mutters, but he throws his hands up in the air, conceding. "All right. Fine. But we're going to talk about that other thing later."

That other thing being me.

Erica will make the decisions for her kids—except me, because I'm not hers anymore. Not according to her and not legally either. She signed away her rights to me when I was four. Granddad had to hire a private investigator to track her down. She was waitressing at some vegetarian café on the Upper East Side while her boyfriend, Isobel's dad, acted in plays off-off-Broadway.

Erica sets her coffee down on the hood of her beat-up silver car and searches through her bag. "Where the hell are the movers? They should be here by now."

I can tell Granddad is biting his tongue. *Language, Erica.*

"Girls, would you like to see your room?" he asks instead. "Ivy can show you."

"I'll do it," Erica says quickly. Like she's worried that if I'm alone with them, I'll spill her secret.

I should. I should tell them right now. *I'm not your aunt. I'm your sister. Your mama's my mama too. She ran out on me when I was a baby. She's a liar and a terrible, selfish person, and you can't trust her. Better you learn that now.*

I step forward. Open my mouth to say it. But then the wind shifts and I'm hit with the scent of strawberry bubble gum. I look down at Gracie's sunny, gap-toothed smile and I can't.

I don't know where Erica would go, but I believe she is just selfish enough to pack the girls back in her car and drive away, and Granddad and I would never see Gracie and Isobel again.

And I want to get to know them. It kind of punches me in the gut how much. Who is Isobel texting? Does she have a boyfriend? Does she play sports or maybe an instrument? Is Gracie obsessed with Disney princesses and dogs like I was at her age, or is she into soccer and nail polish like Abby's little sisters?

Has either of them inherited some marvelous Milbourn talent?

Maybe it's different if you don't grow up here with the weight of all those expectations. But between Isobel's slouch and Gracie's worried eyes, I'm not so sure.

"Are you putting us in my old room?" Erica asks.

Granddad shakes his head. "The girls can have the guest room. The *nursery* last time you were here. Ivy's up in the attic now."

"You get to sleep in an attic?" Gracie asks. "Is it *haunted*?"

Isobel looks up from her phone long enough to roll her eyes. They're like Erica's, big and brown, coated in sparkly purple shadow. "Don't be stupid. There's no such thing as ghosts."

"Iz, don't call your sister stupid," Erica snaps, and Isobel curls into herself.

"No ghosts. We've got a widow's walk though." I point to the roof. "That balcony up there. Have you ever seen one before? We can go watch for the moving truck if you want."

"Can I go see, Mama?" Gracie asks. "Please?"

Erica turns her dark gaze on me. Watching. Weighing. Will I tell?

I stare back, chin up, game face on. But I can't help wondering what she thinks of me.

"All right, Grace," she says after a long moment. "Go ahead. But be careful."

She says it like she cares. Gracie squeals and throws herself at Erica, hugging her around the waist. Erica pats Grace's shoulder, and her face softens when she looks down at her little girl.

"You want to come?" I ask Isobel.

"No," she scoffs. I don't miss the way she glances at her mother afterward, seeking her approval, rewarded when Erica tosses a scrap of a smile her way.

"Suit yourself." I lead the way inside, Gracie skipping after me.

"Izzy's mad because she wanted to stay in DC with Daddy," she confides the second the screen door bangs shut behind us. "She was supposed to go to theater camp and she didn't want to leave her friends. And her *boy*friend." She draws the word *boy* out like it's seventeen syllables long. "You got a boyfriend?"

"Nope." But I think of Connor and his tattoos and the way his eyes trailed over my legs, and I feel myself blushing. "What about you?"

"Ew! No! I'm *six*, silly!" Gracie giggles, climbing the stairs next to me.

"I meant are you okay with being here for the summer?" It must be hard, leaving her father and everything familiar to come live with strangers.

She shrugs. "Daddy says I can visit him on the weekends. Izzy too. Or he'll come and visit us. He says there's a hotel here where you can have a tea party. Like with the *queen*!"

I laugh as I open the attic door. "There is. I've been there." I had my seventh birthday party at the Blue Heron Inn. My friends and I wore poufy dresses and little hats. We thought we were incredibly fancy. Alex was the only boy and Luisa made him wear a suit and he was so mad. Only till he saw all the cookies though. We both ate ourselves sick.

"Is blue your favorite color?" Gracie points at my navy comforter and the navy-and-white-striped curtains. "My favorite color is pink."

"I like pink too. My prom dress was pink." I grab the picture of Alex and me off the nightstand and show her.

Gracie plants her hands on her skinny hips. "You said you didn't have a boyfriend!"

"I don't! This is Alex. He and his mom, Luisa, live in the carriage house in our backyard. Luisa is our housekeeper, and Alex is my best friend. You'll meet them at supper."

"A boy best friend?" Gracie wrinkles her nose as she examines the picture. "Your dress is pretty."

"Thank you." It was bright pink with a V-neck and an A-line skirt that flared out when I twirled, and I twirled a lot that night. Claire went solo, and Abby went with her boyfriend, Ty, a friend of Alex's from the baseball team. The five of us had dinner at the Crab Claw beforehand and went to the bonfire at the cove after. It was a pretty perfect night, right up until the very end.

I guess more-than-friendship had been brewing between Alex and me for a while, but that night it became impossible to ignore. It was there between us when Alex wrapped his arm around me as we posed for a million pictures for Granddad and Luisa, and it was there when we were dancing to a slow song, swaying together with my arms looped around his neck. As we were leaving the dance, he put his hand on the small of my back, guiding me through the crowd, and it felt different. Possessive. Even though we've raced and wrestled and dunked each other about a million times, I suddenly felt so aware of his touch, his thumb brushing against the curve of my hip. Like he was claiming me as *his*.

I wasn't sure I liked it.

Later, when he walked me to my door at three in the morning, he stopped and looked at me. Really *looked*, like I wasn't the Ivy he'd been looking at his whole life—or maybe I was, but I was also more. Ivy-plus. He tucked my hair behind my ear, and his fingers hesitated on my neck. Then he leaned in, and I knew he was going to kiss me.

I ducked away and laughed. Told him his judgment had obviously been impaired by the beers he'd had at the bonfire. Told him we were friends, *best* friends, and I didn't want to screw that up.

Then I ran inside like a third-grader scared of catching cooties.

It felt like the right decision then, and now that I've met my mother, I'm even more relieved that Alex and I are just friends. I don't think I could handle any more big changes this summer.

I pull open the trapdoor in the ceiling and climb the stairs to the widow's walk. Gracie follows me up. The briny air feels good after the stuffy heat of the attic. The white floorboards shine in the sun, surrounded by a waist-high fence. Gracie slides her starry, pink sunglasses back on, and together we squint out over the Bay.

I can see across the channel and down to the Garrettsons' gray house. In the other direction is the old Moudowney place with its red barn and silo. Fields of corn and potatoes and soybeans stretch out like a green-and-gold patchwork quilt. Robert Moudowney was Dorothea's lover—the one she wrote her most famous love poems about. They were in and out of each other's houses when they were kids, then grew up and married other people, and then she took to sneaking over to his law office on Queen Street in the afternoons. She wasn't real discreet about it. Dedicated her last book to him and everything. Granddad used to joke about me and Ian Moudowney getting married, but Ian came out as gay last spring, so that seems unlikely.

Gracie stares at the sun twinkling on the Bay. "Is that where you go swimming?"

"Yep." I wonder if she knows why Erica won't let her swim. I point to the brick carriage house in the backyard. "See that little house? That's where Alex and Luisa live."

Gracie twirls a strand of blond hair around her forefinger. "Does he have any brothers or sisters?"

"Nope. Just him."

Her little mouth twists. "Izzy is a pain, but I'm glad Mama didn't let her stay in DC. I'd miss her too much." She scuffs her pink sneakers against the floorboards. "Weren't you lonely when Mama went to New York?"

Erica ran away in the middle of the night. Left me in the

crib and left a note for Granddad on the kitchen table. Said she just couldn't do it anymore.

Did she mean being his daughter?

Or being my mother?

Seems like she's managed just fine with Isobel and Grace.

Why them and not me? Was there something wrong with me? Something that made her incapable of loving me the way a mother should?

I thought I was long past wondering why she left. Past wanting her to provide the answers. But her showing up here with Gracie and Isobel has brought back all my old questions. Maybe they were there all along, bobbing right under the surface.

Gracie's still waiting for her answer.

"I was real little when your mama left. And I had Granddad and Alex and Luisa. I was okay." I smile down at her. "But I'm glad you and Isobel are here now."

"And Mama," Gracie adds.

"And Mama," I agree. But it tastes like a lie.

CHAPTER
FIVE

THE MOVING VAN COMES AND GOES WITHIN THE HOUR. TWO BURLY men cart boxes marked ERICA and IZ and GRACIE up to the second floor. I offer to help my sisters unpack, but Isobel snaps that they can do it themselves and practically slams the door in my face. The house feels as if it's holding its breath in the calm before a storm, so I hide in my room and reread some Edna St. Vincent Millay. Which poem did Connor love enough to tattoo over his heart?

I can't stop thinking about him, wondering what he thought of me, *if* he's thought of me.

Granddad has another collection of Millay in the library. I'm halfway down the hall when I hear raised voices.

Erica and Granddad are arguing already. And I bet I know what it's about.

I press against the wall, listening.

"Do you think it was *easy* for me to ask you for help? I'd rather bite off my own goddamn tongue. You always thought I'd come back home with my tail between my legs. Well, here I am. I'm broke. No husband, no house, no job. Happy now?"

"I only wanted the best for you, Erica. You may not believe that, but it's true." Granddad sounds bone weary. "I don't think you've thought this through. The girls are going to find out. It's a small town. People gossip."

"Like I could forget." A can pops open. "The things they said about me—about Mom—"

"You can't erase Ivy because she's inconvenient for you," Granddad interrupts. "I won't allow it. If you want to stay, you have to tell Grace and Isobel the truth."

There's a long silence, and then:

"I can't. Rick threatened to take Grace away from me. You might not think I'm much of a mother, but I'm all she has. Girls should be with their mother," she says, and the irony of that does not escape me. "If he knew about Ivy... I will not let that bastard use a mistake I made when I was eighteen against me." Erica is pacing, her stiletto heels drumming against the wooden floor. "I will *not* lose another child."

Lose. Like it was an accident and not a choice she made. Like I'm dead and not right here, ten feet away from her.

"No one took Ivy away from you," Granddad says. "You left. And you can't expect her to perpetuate this lie for you. She has feelings."

"I don't care," my mother says, and the absolute truth of it knocks me breathless. I lean against the cool plaster, dizzy. "Bad enough that we have to live in this goddamn mausoleum all summer. I will not have my girls look at me the way you do. The way *she* does."

Granddad sighs. "And how is that?"

"Like a loser!" Erica bursts out. "What did you tell her about me?"

"Hardly anything," he says. "She's old enough and smart enough to form her own opinions. If she's angry with you, perhaps it's because you deprived her of the chance to know her mother and sisters. Don't you think she has a right to be hurt by that?"

"I was never good enough for you," Erica says.

"That's not true." Their words are quick, familiar, like this part of the fight is a well-trod path. I wonder how many times they've had this argument. "You could have been amazing. You had a gift, Erica, and you threw it away."

"I never wanted it in the first place! And that killed you, didn't it? I was happy singing with the band and being a waitress. I didn't want to go to college. Always liked boys better than school anyhow. You knew that, but you still acted like it was some kind of personal insult when I got knocked up again and dropped out. I was *sick*, Daddy. I was sick and I was sad!"

"You were *selfish*. You walked out on your own child." Granddad's voice is like a whip. "I made some mistakes too. I'll admit that. But Ivy—she's a good girl, Erica. Smart. Healthy. Strong. I can't let you come in here and ruin that."

"Healthy? Please. She's grown up here, hasn't she? With all this?" I can't see through the wall, but I bet Erica is pointing at Grandmother's twisted paintings or at Dorothea's portrait. "With you? I bet she's dying to get out of here."

It takes a second for Erica to realize the cruel double meaning of her words. "I–I didn't mean—"

"Ivy's happy here," Granddad insists.

"Sure." Erica lets out a sour little laugh. "You keep telling yourself that."

My heart pounds. She doesn't know me. She doesn't care whether I'm happy. She's just trying to hurt Granddad, and I will not let her use me as a weapon against him.

I stalk into the library.

"Don't talk about me like you know who I am or what I want." I glare at my mother. "You don't know one single thing about me."

Her gaze meets mine. "I know you're a Milbourn girl,"

she says. "And I remember everything that goes along with that. The lessons. The expectations. The gossip." She raises her eyebrows. "What's your talent, Ivy? What do you do?"

My name in her mouth is like spoiled milk. The question lingers in the air, curdling.

"Nothing. I don't have one," I say flatly.

For once, Granddad doesn't contradict me.

"Really?" Erica's face softens. "Well, good for you."

"Ivy." Granddad reaches out a hand, but I shy away from him. "You don't have to go along with this. It's not fair for her to expect you to lie to your sisters."

But *his* expectations are fair? Asking me to spend the whole summer with the woman who abandoned me?

The traitorous thought winds its way around my heart and squeezes.

Granddad has done everything for me. Raised me. Loved me. If I asked him to choose, he would choose me. He would send them away. I know that.

But this is his chance to make things right with his daughter, no matter how awful she is, and to get to know Isobel and Gracie. I won't take that away from him. I won't be like Erica, putting herself first and not caring about the casualties she leaves in her wake.

I turn back to my mother. "No, it's not fair. But if you want to tell the girls I'm their aunt, you go right ahead. I'm not going to be the one to tell them the truth. It's a stupid plan though." She flinches at the word *stupid*, and I feel a small, petty pleasure at hurting her. We are *far* from even. "People around here have long memories and big mouths. My sisters will find out. And when they do, they'll hate you. Just like I do."

"Ivy—" Granddad catches at my elbow.

I shake him off. "I'm fine. I'm going for a swim. Call me when supper's ready."

I brush past my mother and head out the door, across the backyard, and down the sandy path to the beach. Earlier, I threw on a blue sundress over my bathing suit. Now I shuck it off and dive in. The cold water is a welcome shock.

All my life I've worried I would end up like my mother, but I was wrong.

Erica and I have nothing—*nothing*—in common.

. . . . .

I'm lying on the dock, staring up at the clouds, when Alex comes.

He stands over me, casting a shadow. "Hey. Ma says supper's almost ready."

"You see that cloud?" I point. "Doesn't it look like a bunny rabbit?"

Alex cranes his neck. "Nope."

I huff and sit up. "You have no imagination."

"You have enough for both of us." He plops down next to me. "How's it going?"

"Erica told my sisters I'm their aunt."

"Seriously?" When I nod, he covers my hand with his. His fingers are warm against mine, still cold and pruney from being in the water so long. "What's the Professor going to do?"

I take my hand back and squeeze the water from my ponytail. "He said she has to tell them the truth or they can't stay. She said if we don't go along with it, she'll leave. I told her to go ahead and lie. I don't care. They're going to find out... I just want a chance to get to know my sisters."

Alex is sitting nearer than he needs to. Our knees aren't quite touching, but close. "What are they like?"

I shrug. "Gracie's real cute. Smart too. Isobel's kind of a brat, but I'm not sure how much of it's just for show."

"Well, you won't get to know them if you're hiding out here. Let's go see what Ma made for supper." He stands and pulls me to my feet. I grab my sundress and yank it back over my head.

We walk up to the house and into the kitchen, where Luisa is stirring marinara sauce. Spaghetti bubbles on the stove, and the scent of meatballs—hamburger and oregano and onion—wafts out from the oven. My stomach rumbles.

Alex tries to grab a slice of garlic bread, and Luisa slaps his hand. "Stop that," she says, then turns to me. "How you holding up, baby?"

"Okay." I accept her hug, leaning down because I'm a good eight inches taller. Luisa's brown hair is graying at the temples, there are laugh lines at the corners of her eyes, and she's always saying she'd like to lose twenty pounds. But to me, she's beautiful. She smells like garlic and butter and home.

"Hang in there, Ivy. Will you two set the dining room table? For five," she clarifies, and my shoulders slump. I thought for sure she and Alex would be joining us. She notes my reaction. "Sorry, honey. Just family tonight."

I take out five dinner plates, and she hands me a pile of napkins. She gives Alex a stack of salad plates with silverware piled on top. "I'm not even eating here!" he protests, but he follows me down the hall and into the dining room.

We hardly ever eat in here. Only when there's more company than will fit at the kitchen table. That's what Erica and Isobel and Gracie feel like to me: company, not family.

Light streams in from the floor-to-ceiling windows, which open onto the wraparound porch. The effect should be airy and lovely, but it's ruined by two of Grandmother's sinister paintings. In one, gulls are caught in an updraft above savage, dark waves. In the other, the Bay has flooded its banks and filled our backyard after some big storm. .

For the billionth time, I wonder why Granddad doesn't sell these. When he looks at them, does he still see Grandmother's talent instead of her sickness? *How?*

"Sorry I can't stay for supper," Alex says.

"It's stupid. You are too family. More than they are."

He hip checks me as we move around the table. "Not really."

"Technically, no. But you *know* me." I fold the napkins into swans. It's a catering trick Abby taught me. I bet Gracie will get a kick out of it. "They're strangers. And they don't like me."

"They don't know you yet. Once they get to know you, they'll love you." Alex arranges the last couple of forks. "You kinda have that effect on people."

On people in general? Or on him? Does Alex mean *he* loves me?

The thought sends a wave of panic rolling through me.

I mean, of course he loves me. I love him too. He's my best friend. That's all he means, right? So much is changing this summer; I need Alex and me to stay the same as we've always been.

Luisa bustles in, carrying a big glass pitcher of sweet tea. Granddad follows with the basket of garlic bread. Just as the grandfather clock in the corner begins to chime six, Gracie runs down the stairs. Erica and Isobel follow her, and we all stand clustered in the front hall, surrounded by pictures of Dorothea.

"This is Luisa Garcia, our housekeeper, and her son, Alex," Granddad says. "Luisa, Alex, this is my daughter Erica, and my granddaughters, Gracie and Isobel."

"It's nice to meet you." Luisa smiles. "I'm going for groceries tomorrow. If there's anything special you'd like, let me know and I'll pick it up for you. If you have any food allergies—"

"We're not fancy," Erica interrupts, her lipstick a slash of red in her unsmiling face. "No special requests. We're used to cooking and cleaning up after ourselves like normal people do."

"It's really no trouble." Luisa smiles, but I can tell she's flustered as she runs a hand over the apple-print apron I gave her a few years ago for Mother's Day.

I look at Alex, embarrassed that my mom is so awful, and he moves closer, his shoulder knocking into mine. His navy-blue Cecil Warriors Baseball T-shirt is soft against my bare arm.

"Luisa started taking care of us when Ivy was little." *When you left*, Granddad might as well say. "We'd be lost without her. I'm useless in the kitchen. Ivy's getting to be a great cook though."

The timer for the meatballs goes off, and Luisa steps away. I rush to fill the awkward silence. "I like to bake, mostly. I was thinking maybe I could make a strawberry pie for dessert tomorrow night. If you want." I look at Gracie. "You like strawberries, right?"

"I love strawberries!" Gracie tugs on her big sister's arm. "Izzy likes to bake too. She makes the *best* chocolate-chip cookies."

"Iz could stand to lay off the chocolate-chip cookies," Erica mutters, and Isobel flushes and yanks on the hem of her T-shirt.

I bite my lip. I cannot *believe* Erica just said that.

Isobel's curvy, not all angles like Erica and Gracie. But she's not fat. Even if she were fat, who cares? It still wouldn't be okay to police what she eats and shame her in front of everyone.

"Well, you're welcome to use the kitchen any time, Isobel. Luisa keeps it pretty well stocked, but if there's anything else you need, you just let us know," Granddad says.

"I don't need anything. I'm on a diet," Isobel croaks. Her brown eyes are fixed on the floor like she wishes she could melt right through it.

Fury rises in me. She's beautiful the way she is. There's more to being pretty—or healthy—than being skinny.

But I don't know her, and I don't want to say the wrong thing and make her feel worse.

Gracie is staring at Alex. "You're Aunt Ivy's friend who's a boy but not her boyfriend, right?"

Alex winces at *Aunt Ivy*, but he recovers fast. "Yep, that's me."

"She showed me a picture of you. Daddy says boys don't wear pink, but I like your tie. It matched Ivy's dress!"

Alex chuckles. "Thanks. That was the idea."

"Alex is the first baseman for the Warriors," Granddad brags. "Got a couple colleges already scouting him. And he made honor roll last semester too."

Alex shoves his hands in the pockets of his cargo shorts. "Ivy's the smart one. Third in our class."

"Of course she is," Erica says.

I freeze. *What does she mean by that?*

Granddad's jaw twitches. "Ivy works hard."

I do work hard. I study my ass off. And he means it as a compliment, but I only hear how it's not enough. Third place, not salutatorian, not valedictorian.

Luisa leans out of the kitchen. "Dinner's ready, if you're hungry."

"We're going out for pizza," Erica says. "Come on, girls."

Granddad's face falls. "Erica, stay. Please. Luisa went to the trouble of making a nice supper to welcome you all home."

Erica pivots on one stiletto heel. "This isn't my home. I *hate* this house." She slams a hand against the wall, and the photo of Dorothea getting her Pulitzer crashes to the floor. The glass shatters. Everyone flinches.

"Mama, I want to stay here and eat with Granddad and Aunt Ivy," Gracie says.

"Smart girl," Alex says. "Ma's spaghetti and meatballs are the best."

"Alex." Luisa beckons him from the kitchen. "Stay out of it. Let's go."

Alex touches my arm. "You're still coming to the bonfire, right? Pick you up at nine?"

"Bonfire?" Erica raises her perfectly arched eyebrows. "You're kidding. You let her go to parties at the cove?"

Granddad nods, jaw tight. "I trust Ivy. She's never given me any reason not to."

"Unlike me, you mean." She purses her glossy red lips and grabs a set of keys from her bag. "Come on, girls. Let's go."

"But Mama! Spaghetti and meatballs is my *favorite*," Gracie whines.

"You can get some at Giovanni's. Now, Grace. I can't breathe in here." Erica holds the door open and the girls scramble out and she slams the door behind her. Leaving Alex and Luisa and Granddad and me staring at each other in horrified silence.

Jesus. What a mess.

· · · · ·

The little cove down from the Crab Claw is packed. The flickering light from the bonfire casts shadows over couples cuddled up on sun-faded beach blankets and big pieces of driftwood. Somebody's speakers blare a country song about getting drunk and kissing a girl in the back of a pickup truck. A few just-graduated seniors are dancing barefoot in the pebbly sand, hands in the air. Guys from the baseball team are drinking Natty Boh and roasting hot dogs. As we get closer, I lose the scent of summer nights on the Shore—brackish water and wet grass—and inhale smoke and beer and cheap cologne.

I am already having doubts about this.

Abby grabs me the minute we arrive. "You came! And you look so cute!" she squeals, pointing at my yellow sundress and green flip-flops with lemons and limes printed on them. My hair falls in loose waves around my shoulders, and I took the time to put on lip gloss and mascara. I do look cute. But she takes another look and hands me a bottle of lemonade. "Here. I think you need this more than I do."

"Lemonade?" I ask.

"Spiked with vodka. You can hardly taste it," she promises, whirling away and snagging a can of beer from the communal cooler. "Want to go for a walk? You look like you need to talk."

We leave Alex with his baseball bros and head toward the mouth of the cove. A rocky point separates the beach from the marina and the Crab Claw. We clamber over the rocks, me clutching on to Abby because my flip-flops are all slippery. On the other side, the night air smells like fish and salt and fried food. There's still a trace of music from the party, but now I hear the slap of waves against the dock and the creaking of sailboats moored in the marina.

I can't count how many times Abby and Claire and I have snuck over here during parties to talk. Mostly they do the talking—about their family problems and their boy problems—and I listen.

Something tells me this summer's going to be different, and I'm not sure how I feel about that. I've always been comfortable listening. Advising. Talking about my own feelings? Spilling my fears? Not so much. Not even with Abby and Claire.

We walk down to the end of the first dock, where a couple big sailboats are moored. I kick off my shoes and sit, dangling my feet out over the dark water. Abby leans against a wooden piling, facing me, cross-legged. She's wearing red shorts—part of her waitressing uniform—but she changed out of her official Crab Claw polo into a white tank top.

I twist off the cap and take a sip of lemonade.

She's right. I really can't taste the vodka. I gulp down more.

"That bad?" Abby asks.

"Want to steal one of these boats and run away from home?"

She makes a face. "Don't tempt me." Things have been hard at her house too, ever since last fall when her little brother, Eli, started wanting to wear dresses to kindergarten. It wasn't entirely out of nowhere; he'd always had his hair long and worn his big sisters' clothes and makeup around the house. Abby's mom has been really supportive of what she calls his *gender expression*. Abby's dad, not so much. Abby and her other sisters feel caught in the middle, wanting to support Eli but struggling to understand and worrying about how kids at school will treat him.

"How's Eli?" I ask.

"He started asking us to call him Ella. Dad is *not* having it. Every time one of us says 'she' instead of 'he,' he freaks the hell out. He and Mom had a huge fight about it last night." Abby pulls her blond hair into a long ponytail. "How's your mom?"

"Kind of a bitch. Granddad is doing her a kindness by letting her come home, and she's picking fights with everybody. Him. Me. Even Luisa, who's never done anything to her."

Neither have I, I remind myself. *Unless you count being born.*

Abby frowns. "What did she say to you?"

"She told me I was tall." I take another drink. "Her first words to me in fifteen years were, 'Jesus, you're tall.'"

"Seriously?" Abby fiddles with the silver infinity

necklace Ty gave her, her blue eyes sympathetic. "And then what?"

"She told my sisters I'm their aunt. Her little sister."

"She *what*?" Abby gasps.

"Yep. Gracie calls me 'Aunt Ivy.'" I relate the whole awful conversation in the library, punctuating my story with sips of lemonade. "Hearing her say straight up that she doesn't care about my feelings, that I was a mistake—"

"You were not. *She* made the mistake when she left. *She* missed out, because you're awesome," Abby says. "You know that, right?" Her phone beeps but she doesn't look at it. "*Right?*"

I nod, but my throat is tight because I don't feel entirely convinced.

Her phone beeps again, and this time she glances at it and her whole face lights up. "Ty's here!"

I wish I had somebody who made me smile like that.

Like a mind reader, Abby nudges me. "Hey, you know what I bet would make you feel better? Making out with Alex."

Ever since I told her how Alex almost kissed me after prom, she's been relentless. She loves the idea of her and Ty and Alex and me double-dating, of us going to the movies and parties and cheering the boys on at their baseball games. But we do all those things already.

Abby means well, but I am tired of everyone telling me

who I am, who I should be, what I should want. Who I date—if I date anybody at all—is going to be my own choice. "How many times do I have to tell you that Alex is like my brother?"

"Right. Your hot brother you want to make out with, maybe." Abby drains her beer. "Like *Flowers in the Attic*."

"Jesus," I mutter, but I can't help laughing. "Go back to the party and see your boy."

She tilts her head. "You sure? I can stay. We can talk more."

"It's okay. I need some time."

She and Claire are used to me being an introvert. Granddad calls me "Ivy Bear," but Claire and Abby tease that I'm more like a prickly little hedgehog. Abby squeezes my shoulder. "Okay. See you in a few," she says and bounces off.

Once she's gone, I slump against the wooden piling and stare at the sailboats silhouetted against the dark water.

This was a mistake. I should've stayed home and read a book instead of inflicting myself on other people. I don't want to pretend to be fine, pretend that I'm not reeling and angry and sad.

I finish my drink, then haul myself up and head back to the party. At the mouth of the marina, wooden benches line the brick sidewalk, which follows the arc of the shore. By the end of the night, a couple of the benches will be filled with couples making out.

I feel a tug of yearning. I don't want to mess up my friendship with Alex, but it'd be nice to be one of those couples. To have someone to kiss and touch.

As I round the corner, I see that one of the benches is occupied. Not by a couple. Just one guy, drinking what looks like a beer. I squint through the dark to see if it's anybody I know, and then I grin.

Connor Clarke is sitting there in khaki shorts and a brick-red T-shirt, like I conjured him right out of thin air.

I remember him checking me out. Twice.

This a bad idea, Ivy, whispers a little voice in my head. *Find another boy. This one's too complicated.*

I ignore it.

CHAPTER
SIX

CONNOR LIFTS HIS BOTTLE IN GREETING. "IVY, HEY."

I approach cautiously, like he's some wild bird I might spook. "Hey. What's up?"

He shrugs. "Roommate said I couldn't miss the first bonfire of the summer."

The first bonfire of the summer was after prom, and the second was last week, after graduation. But I don't correct him because those were high school parties and I guess I don't want to remind him that I'm still in high school.

I gesture back toward the cove. "Party's over there. What're you doing over here by yourself?"

As soon as the words are out of my mouth, it occurs to me that maybe he's waiting for someone. Like a girlfriend.

"I didn't want to bail on Josh, but I'm not really in the mood for a party," he says, and my mind races. Maybe he *had* a girlfriend and she broke up with him. Maybe he needs someone to console him. Maybe I could be that person.

"Me either." I play with the empty lemonade bottle, peeling the label a little, but Abby claims that somehow signals you are sexually frustrated, so I get self-conscious and stop.

"Professor said he was taking a few days off to deal with some family stuff. Everything okay?" Connor gestures to the empty space beside him.

I sit, angling myself toward him. He looks like he actually cares, so I feel kind of obliged not to blow off the question. "Nobody's sick or anything. Just…my mother's in town. She and Granddad don't have the best relationship."

Connor nods. "He mentioned that he and his daughter are estranged."

I give a short, sour laugh. *Estranged.* Such a polite word. "She ran off when I was two years old. Granddad raised me. Today was the first time we've seen her since."

"Holy shit." Connor's gaze lands on the empty bottle in my lap. "And you're drinking lemonade?"

"With some vodka in it." I give him a bashful smile. "What about you? Why are you drinking all by yourself? Or…you don't have to tell me if you don't want to talk about it."

"It's okay." He sets his empty bottle down on the sidewalk. "My grams is sick. Alzheimer's. It sucks. My mom called and said Grams didn't recognize her today. Called her Bess, who was Grams's sister. Mom cried when she was telling me about it. And she's not a crier." His hand clenches into a fist on his knee, and I notice his fingers are ink-splattered again.

"That's… Jesus. I'm sorry." I can't imagine losing Granddad like that, little by little, bit by bit. "Are you and your grams close?"

"Yeah. She babysat my sister and me when we were little, while my parents were at work." He swallows. "She was diagnosed last year, so it's not unexpected, I guess. But it's hard. Especially on my mom. At first she'd forget little things, you know? Her keys or whatnot. I think she hid it from us for a while. Didn't want to lose her independence. But now? Now she'll have the same conversations over and over. She can remember stuff that happened thirty, forty years ago, no problem, but not what happened yesterday. When I went home a couple weekends ago, she played it like she knew who I was, but I don't think she did. At least not at first."

"That must be hard." I go to touch his forearm, just a friendly gesture of sympathy, but I chicken out and let my hand fall on my own knee instead.

Connor nods. "My great-granddad had it too. It scares

the shit out of me, thinking my mom could inherit that. Or me. I've always had a good memory. I even won this contest back in high school for reciting poetry. I can't imagine reaching for words and not having them there."

I fiddle with my ring, which has a little gold hedgehog on it. Claire gave it to me for my birthday. Thinking of Claire gives me courage. "That's a writer's worst nightmare, not being able to find the words for things. Not being able to communicate."

"You know 'Dirge Without Music'?" He waits for me to nod, and I do. It's one of my favorite Millay poems. He taps a spot on his chest right above his heart. "I got a tattoo with a couple lines from it when I was home over winter break. When I saw how Grams had started going downhill. I was so *mad*."

I recite the first line, showing off a little. Connor doesn't seem to mind. He joins in. I only know the first stanza, so I trail off and listen as he recites the rest. It might seem crazy pretentious coming from someone else, but hearing him recite this poem—knowing what it means to him—it feels intimate.

"I love that poem," I say when he's finished.

"Me too." He gives a self-deprecating smile. "Obviously, I guess."

I smile back, gesturing at the tattoo on his forearm. "Can I see?"

"Sure." He flips his arm over, revealing some lines from Langston Hughes. I reach out, tracing my fingers lightly over the words, over his smooth, brown skin, a little surprised by my own boldness. "How many tattoos do you have?"

"Six so far." He points to Dorothea's poem on his bicep, then the Millay lines over his heart, and then tugs up his shirt to reveal words printed on his lower abdomen.

Jesus, he is cut. He actually has that vee that disappears into the waistband of his boxers, which I have previously only seen on TV. The vee, I mean, not his boxers. His boxers are blue plaid. Why I am thinking about his boxers?

I drag my eyes back up to his without reading the lines from the poem. All I can think about is tracing that ink with my fingers. "Nice," I murmur.

He smiles a little, like he knows that I am admiring more than the tattoo.

He lets his shirt fall. "And two on my back. How about you?"

"Me what?" My brain is fuzzy, and it has nothing to do with the vodka.

"Any tattoos?" His pretty, tawny eyes scan me from head to toe, and I am suddenly conscious of how much of my own skin is showing. I'm hardly modest; I'm used to being in my swimsuit all the time. But now every uncovered inch of me feels different. Flushed and—waiting. Wanting.

I remember his question and shake my head. Granddad would have a fit if I got a tattoo. But Connor's in college. He's at least eighteen, maybe nineteen. He doesn't need his parents' permission for things anymore.

"Maybe someday. I don't know what I'd get though. Or where I'd put it."

Connor looks at me—like, really takes his sweet time looking—and then leans in. I hold my breath as his hand brushes butterfly soft just below my collarbone. "A tattoo would look good here." My skin goes shivery at his touch despite the sultry summer air. Sometimes I worry my shoulders are too broad, too muscled. I like that he thinks I should show them off.

I can't even breathe with how much I want to kiss him. The air between us goes electric. I lean in and he dips his head and then we are kissing, his mouth moving softly against mine. My eyes flutter closed. He tastes like beer and I don't even mind. His hand moves to the back of my head, his fingers tugging a little in my hair.

Tentatively, I slide a hand up his arm. His other hand slides down my spine, and it makes me shiver in the best way. We kiss and kiss and he tries to tug me closer, but it's impossible sitting side by side on this stupid bench with our knees in the way. Our kisses grow harder, hungrier. Ravenous. I want to be closer.

I gather the courage to kick off my flip-flops and swing one leg over his lap so that I'm straddling him. My dress inches up. Connor pulls back to look at me for a second, surprised but not displeased, and then I launch myself at him, kissing him hard. He makes a little groan at the back of his throat, and I am thrilled by my own power. One of his hands slides up my thigh and the other skims up over my ribs, grazing the side of my breast, and I know we are in public, but I want him to touch me.

"Ivy," he says, and the sound of my name on his tongue is so hot. I never knew someone just *looking* at me could make my stomach flip, could make my whole body react like this.

Our lips meet again and my hair falls down around us in a tangled brown curtain, shielding our faces, creating our own little private bubble. Then the wind blows and Connor laughs, swiping a strand of my hair out of his mouth. I giggle too. I pull an elastic off my wrist and yank my hair into a quick ponytail. Then I blush as I realize that from this angle, me perched on top of him, he can see right down my dress. I'm glad I'm wearing a cute yellow bra.

But I'm not a little pixie like Abby. Suddenly, I feel self-conscious. "Is this okay? Am I crushing you?"

Connor shakes his head. "It's way more than okay." He sits up a little, holding me close with a hand at the small of my back. His mouth moves to my neck, which feels incredible, and I slide closer—close enough that I can tell he is as into this as I am, in case I had any doubts. I wonder what it would be like if we were somewhere private, how far we would let this go.

"*Ivy?*" Alex is standing a few feet away, a beer in his hand and a look on his face I've never seen before. He is *pissed*. I pull away from Connor, untangling my arms from around his neck, scrambling off his lap.

"What... Who the hell is this?" Alex demands.

I tug my dress down. I can still feel the warm imprint of Connor's hand on my thigh. "Hey. Hi. Um, this is Connor."

Connor gives him a head nod, running a hand over his close-cropped hair. "Uh, hey."

Alex ignores him, leaning over and picking up my empty lemonade bottle, which has rolled away from the bench. He looks from it to me like he's putting puzzle pieces together. "Ivy, are you *drunk?*"

"No!" I step back into my flip-flops.

"Right. Nice. You didn't notice she was drunk, or you didn't care?" He glares at Connor and grabs my elbow. "Come on. I'm taking you home."

I yank away. "Wait a minute. Don't make it sound like that. It's not... It wasn't like that." I look back at Connor, whose eyes are narrowed as he watches Alex and me. I want to be clear. I might have let things go further than I should have in public, but I wanted this to happen. I was a very enthusiastic participant.

"You sure about that? This isn't like you. I know it's been a rough day," Alex says in a low voice, and for a second I *hate* him. Hate that he knows me so well, that he can say so authoritatively what is and isn't like me. "Come on, Ivy. Let me take you home."

Connor stands. Alex is tall, but Connor is taller. Broader. My eyes trace his shoulders, where my hands rested just a few minutes ago. His lower lip, which I was biting a minute ago. "Wait, Ivy—"

Alex turns on him. "Leave her alone."

"Look, I don't know who you are," Connor says, "but I'd like to hear from Ivy what she wants to do."

I blush as I step between them. "Connor, this is my… Alex," I say. How to explain it? Ivy and Alex, Alex and Ivy. "My friend."

"Your friend?" Connor looks from Alex to me like he's trying to figure out whether we might be more than friends. Given how Alex is acting, I can't blame him. "Do you want him to take you home?"

No. I want to stay here and kiss away every thought of what's happening at home. But the spell is broken. "I… What time is it?" I dig my phone out of my pocket—bless dresses with pockets—and check the time. We've been kissing for a while. Long enough that it's getting close to my curfew. "Gah. I should get home. I'm sorry. Granddad can be a little…" I trail off, biting my lip. Connor is his *student*.

Connor's gaze fastens on my mouth. He catches me catching him and grins. "Yeah. I got the sense the Professor is, uh—protective."

I shrug. "He's all I've got."

It comes out sounding sadder than I'd intended.

"That's not true," Alex says. It's a nice sentiment, but he isn't saying it to make me feel less lonely. He's staking his claim.

I ignore him and look up at Connor. "I'm really sorry. Not about…just…" I flail. *I'm sorry we were interrupted. Sorry I have to go. Not sorry for kissing you.* But I can't make the words come out. Not with Alex standing right behind me, listening. "'Night, Connor."

"'Night, Ivy," he echoes, flashing me another grin.

It fades when Alex grabs my hand and pulls me back toward the beach.

I wait until we are out of earshot because, unlike my mother, I do not relish making a scene. But when we near the rocks that lead back to the cove and the party, I yank my hand away and stop dead. "What the hell was that, Alex? What were you doing back there?"

"Me?" He laughs and drains the rest of his beer. "What about you?"

I plant my hands on my hips. "Whatever I was doing or not doing with Connor is none of your business."

"Are you serious?" Alex stares at me. "I came looking for you because you were gone so long. I was *worried* about you. And I found you half-drunk and making out with some stranger. You honestly expect me to just turn around and walk away?"

"Yes! No. I don't know. I'm not drunk. And he's not a stranger. He's one of Granddad's students. He was at the house the other day for lunch."

"Oh, well, that makes it okay then! I'm sure the Professor would be real happy about it."

I draw a deep breath in through my teeth. Count to ten. Twice. It doesn't help much.

"Let's get something straight right now." My voice is so cold it doesn't sound like mine. "It is not your place to say whether or not it's okay, and it isn't Granddad's either. Who I kiss is my own damn business. You don't get any say in that."

I scramble back over the rocks to the beach, stumbling in my flip-flops and banging the shit out of my knee.

"Ivy!" Alex calls, but I ignore him and hurry across the sand. The music is blasting and a couple guys are chugging beers while the crowd chants and the bonfire sends sparks spinning up into the night sky.

"Ivy, slow down. Let me walk you home." Alex jogs ahead of me and stops in my path. "I'm sorry, okay? I was trying to stop you from making a mistake. You're upset about Erica and—"

I throw my hands up in the air. "You don't get it. I didn't kiss Connor because of Erica. I didn't kiss him because I was drunk. I just wanted to kiss him, okay? *I wanted to kiss him.* It wasn't a mistake."

Alex takes a step back. "So kissing this dude wasn't a mistake, but kissing *me* after prom would've been?"

Shit.

Not all of my anger evaporates, but a good bit of it does, because I know what Alex sounds like when he's hurting— and it sounds like this.

I hurt him.

"Is that what this is about?" My voice is softer now.

"I've been waiting for you to change your mind," Alex says. "Nobody would treat you better than me. Nobody knows you better."

"Maybe I don't want somebody who already knows me," I say. I say it fast, without thinking, and it's only in that moment that I realize it's true. That's the reason behind all my excuses. I love Alex. Always have, always will. But the only times I've wanted to kiss him were when he looked at me like I was a little bit new.

CHAPTER
SEVEN

MY WORDS HANG UNANSWERED IN THE AIR BETWEEN US. I LOOK away, pretending fascination with the star-drenched sky above us, with the soft, slow shush of the tide washing in.

When I can't stand the silence another minute, I look at Alex. His jaw is clenched; his brown eyes are narrowed. "For somebody who's worked so hard to be nothing like your mom, you're sure acting a lot like her."

I shrink away as though he's slapped me. That's the problem with fighting with your best friends. They know the words that will hurt you most.

You hurt him first, my conscience needles. But that doesn't justify what he said.

Or is Alex telling the truth? Drinking, making out with

someone I barely know—those are the kind of reckless, impulsive choices I've been warned against all my life. They're the choices my mother made. That a Milbourn girl *would* make.

Connor made me feel pretty and smart and *wanted*. Is that so wrong?

"What the fuck did you just say to her?"

Claire sails between us like an avenging goddess. Her sundress is short and fire-engine red, her gold platform wedges are a good four inches high, and the look on her face says she's about two seconds from throwing her drink in his face.

"Stay out of it. This is between Ivy and me," Alex mutters.

"Not anymore." Claire stands tall, without wobbling, and as a girl of flip-flops and ballet flats and sneakers, this impresses me. She props one hand on her hip and stares at Alex with her big, unblinking brown eyes. Waiting for an explanation.

He falters beneath that gaze. Most people do.

"She was kissing some guy. Some college guy. And she's drunk," he says.

"And?" Claire retorts. "You've never gotten drunk and hooked up with somebody? What about Ginny West last Fourth of July? Or Madison's cousin on Labor Day weekend? Or Charlotte Wu at Dave's Halloween party?"

"Wait, Charlotte Wu?" I ask. I heard the gossip about the

girls Alex hooked up with last summer. *Everybody* heard about Ginny. She was a just-graduated senior, two years older than us, and the guys on the baseball team were gross about Alex "scoring a triple" until Claire overheard and shut them down. She and Alex have been sniping at each other ever since.

But Charlotte is on the swim team with me. We used to be friends. This could explain why she froze me out all last season. I thought she was mad because I kept beating her in the one-hundred-meter freestyle, but maybe she was mad that Alex hooked up with her and then never pursued anything. Maybe she thought he wasn't pursuing her because of me.

"Didn't know you were keeping score, Claire," Alex says.

She rolls her eyes. "Don't flatter yourself. I don't care who you hook up with. I'm just making a point. How come what's good for the gander isn't good for the goose?"

Alex squints at her. "What the hell is a gander?"

"A male goose, asshole!" Claire throws up her hands, sloshing white wine out of her cup. "My point is, you're saying it's not okay for Ivy to hook up because she's a girl, and that's some sexist bullshit."

"No, I'm saying it's not okay for Ivy to hook up because it's *Ivy!*"

"Ivy gets to make her own decisions, Alex. Just because she hurt your feelings making out with some other guy doesn't mean you get to be all judgy."

Ouch. People see Claire's short skirts and long legs and they assume she's dumb, but she can suss out in two minutes what it took me an entire conversation to see.

"You know how Ivy feels about her mom. You owe her an apology."

"Forget it," Alex says, red faced, and stalks off.

I sigh. "Claire. That wasn't very nice."

She flips her long, dark hair over her shoulder. "I don't give a shit about being nice."

She really doesn't. I envy that sometimes.

"I know you can defend yourself," she continues. "But I heard what he said about your mom and I saw the look on your face. That was not a cool thing for him to say. Today of all days. You know it's not true, right?"

I bite my lip. "Right."

Claire raises one eyebrow. I've always been jealous she can do that. "Did you have sex with this guy?" she asks.

"No! Jesus! We were just kissing!" Having sex would be skipping several steps for me.

"And he wasn't pressuring you? You were into it?"

I think about Connor's hand on my thigh and his mouth on mine, and a shiver runs down the back of my neck that has nothing to do with the breeze coming off the Bay. "Um. Yes. Very."

Claire laughs her full, throaty laugh. "Oh my God, you're blushing! Ivy! Okay, I want to hear more about this in a minute. But look, you actually had fun for once! That's okay. Don't let Alex make you feel bad about it."

I frown, a little stung. "Are you saying I'm not usually fun?"

"No, I'm saying you'd usually rather be home reading a book than at one of these parties," she says, and she is not wrong. She links an arm through mine. "Come on. I'll walk you home."

I look down at her gold platform wedges. "You're going to walk a mile in those shoes?"

"I'd walk *ten* miles in these shoes for you. Besides," she says, shimmying a little, "they make my ass look fabulous."

. . . . .

It's almost midnight. Most of the old colonial houses along Water Street are dark. My flip-flops thwack on the uneven brick sidewalks. We're halfway through the park, crossing a wooden bridge over a marshy inlet, when Claire lets out a yelp and yanks me to a stop. She points into the marsh, where a big blue heron stands, its eyes glinting in the moonlight.

"Ivy!" Claire whimpers, gripping my forearm with pinching fingers as the bird turns its head to stare at us. She's terrified of birds, even Abby's sisters' parakeet.

It takes several minutes for me to convince her that this

four-foot-tall blue heron is not going to peck us with its long bill or chase us with its long legs, and then she literally runs across the bridge like there might be trolls beneath.

I laugh. It's weirdly reassuring to know that Claire is scared of *something*, even if it is waterfowl. She's so brave most of the time. Like last January when Logan McIntyre told everyone that she gave him head on New Year's Eve. When she realized why everyone was whispering, she didn't go home sick or cry in the girls' bathroom. She went right up to him between chem and English and announced that at least she'd had the class to keep it to herself that the good Lord only gave him two inches.

Then this past spring, she revived the dormant Gay-Straight Alliance at school and came out as bisexual. That earned her a lot of shit about how she's a slut who's down for anything. She said their ignorance only made her more passionate about sex education, so this summer she's volunteering at the women's clinic outside town, even though it means getting insulted and having to walk past posters of fetuses coming and going.

It sucks that Claire had to deal with any of that. But sometimes I envy that she knows what she wants. Sometimes it feels like everybody knows but me. Claire wants to get the hell out of Cecil, to go to American University in DC and major in women's, gender, and sexuality studies. Spend a year abroad in London or Paris or Rome. Abby wants

to go to the University of Maryland and study elementary education while Ty gets his degree in business. Then
they'll get married and come back to Cecil, where he'll
help run his dad's hardware store and she'll teach first grade
and they'll have three kids. She even has the names picked
out! Alex doesn't have his future quite as mapped out, but
he wants to stay in Cecil and play baseball.

And Connor—I remember how passionate Connor was
as he recited the Millay poem.

The only thing that turns me on that much is *him*.

·····

When I fit my key into the back door, it's ten minutes
after twelve. The only sounds are the cicadas in the trees
and the soft lap of waves against the shore. The house
is dark and quiet, and I'm relieved that no one's waited
up for me.

Inside, I kick off my flip-flops and pour a glass of water
by the light of the stove.

"You're late." Granddad's voice floats out of the darkness.

Startled, I smack my hip on the counter and cuss, then
walk down the hall into the library. The lights are all off
and I can barely make him out in the gloom, his white
polo shirt stark against his leather recliner. I lean over and
switch on the lamp. "You waited up for me?" He's hardly

a night owl, and by the end of last summer, I thought he trusted me.

"Wanted to make sure you were all right. We didn't get a chance to talk, just the two of us, before you left." A book is propped open on his chest, like he drifted off at some point. He's still wearing his reading glasses.

"I'm fine. Sorry I'm late." It's not like I rolled in at dawn, but Granddad's a stickler for curfew. "Claire walked me home and we ran into a heron. You know how she is about birds."

Granddad returns the recliner to its upright position and sets his book on the end table. "Claire? Where's Alex?"

"Still at the party." I lean against the doorjamb, arms crossed over my chest.

Granddad doesn't let it go. "You two have a fight?"

"Sort of. It was nice of you to wait up, but I'm tired. Can we talk tomorrow?" I am skirting the edge of politeness, but I cannot bear another confrontation or another discussion about my mother.

Granddad stands, stretches, and strides toward me. "I know this wasn't an easy day, Ivy. It will get better. Erica just needs some time to settle in, feel accepted."

I bite my lip, stung by the implied criticism. "I'm *trying*."

"Not you, honey. That's not what I meant. It's me. She feels I'm still treating her like a child, and here she is with children of her own. She doesn't want me coming between her and the girls. So she's trying to assert herself."

"Assert herself?" I let out a little laugh. "She was a straight-up bitch to everyone."

"Language, Ivy," Granddad chides. "I'm not asking you to like her or even respect her. But we need to keep things civil, at least in front of the girls. She's their mother and… Well, I really do think she's doing her best."

"What if her best isn't good enough?" I ask. "What if they'd be better off with her ex?"

Granddad runs a tired hand over his chin. "I don't know. I think we owe her a little time."

"I don't owe her *anything*," I snap.

He sighs. "You're right. I misspoke. *I* owe her this. And I'm sorry if that seems unfair to you." He pulls me into a hug. I lean on his shoulder and let out a sigh. I can give him this, this chance at a reunion. It's just a few months. I can be selfless that long. Can't I?

Granddad stiffens and pulls back, his blue eyes narrowing. "Have you been drinking?"

There's no point in lying. "Little bit." I lift my chin. "Nothing for you to worry about, I promise."

"I do worry. That's my job." He glances out the french doors toward the carriage house. "Is that what you and Alex were arguing about?"

"No, that was—" What am I supposed to say? *That was because I was making out with your work-study student and Alex got jealous.* I can hardly tell him *that*. "The fight Alex and

I had tonight... It was a long time coming. I really don't want to talk about it."

I blink away sudden tears. I was stupid to think things could stay the same, Ivy and Alex, Alex and Ivy. I knew how he felt. Keeping him at arm's length was only going to keep him there for so long.

Granddad frowns. "Well, you know how I feel about you drinking. I suppose it might not be realistic, expecting a girl your age not to have a drink now and again, but your mother... A lot of the poor choices she's made were because she was abusing alcohol. She didn't come right out and say it, but I gather that was part of the reason she was fired from her last job. Milbourn women never do things in moderation. So there's a history there."

He sighs and rubs the bridge of his nose. "I know this is a lot to handle. Having your mother here, and your sisters, and her telling them what she did. I thought I'd made it clear, but Erica—she never was very good at following directions. If this is all too much for you—"

"It's not. I'm fine." I don't know how many other ways I can say it. "Really. We'll get through this. It's just for the summer, right?"

"You're a good girl, Ivy. Got a good head on your shoulders. But this is asking a lot of you. Maybe too much. I don't know." Granddad stares at the portrait of Dorothea like she might offer some advice. "You never did like to ask me for help. Even when you were little, you were always determined to do everything on your own. I'd hate to see Erica's visit throw you off track. Maybe we should set up some plans for you. Keep you busy. Focused."

I open my mouth to protest, then snap it shut. I want to prove I'm nothing like Erica, don't I? That I can handle responsibility without running away from it?

"What did you have in mind?"

Granddad steeples his fingers together. "How would you feel about a part-time job? You'd get paid, and you could work your hours around your time at the library and the pool."

My mind goes straight to the English department. To Amelia. Maybe she needs help with something Austen or Bronte related, a research assistant to read through dusty old documents on interlibrary loan. I am intrigued. "Tell me more."

"Well, next spring is the fiftieth anniversary of the publication of *Second Kiss*." *Second Kiss* was Dorothea's sixth collection of poems, the one that won her the Pulitzer Prize. "I'm putting together a festival up at the college, but it's coming together more slowly than I'd like. Not much money in the budget, unfortunately. One of the big projects is transcribing all her journals to add them to the online archives."

He gestures to the bookshelves that hold Dorothea's

seven collections of poetry, their foreign translations, and—on the bottom two rows—almost four dozen leather-bound journals filled with her spidery handwriting. She started keeping a diary when she was sixteen, right after the accident that killed her mother and sisters, and the last entry is dated the day she was murdered.

"I'd hoped to transcribe them myself, but with this arthritis—" Granddad flexes his swollen fingers with a pained grimace. "And you know I hate that dictation software. What do you think?"

"I think I'd love to help, actually. I can already read her handwriting." Three summers ago, I spent most of July reading through the journals. Granddad wouldn't let me take them out of the library, much less outside the house, so I lay on the cool hardwood floor, with the ceiling fan spinning lazily overhead, and read them one right after the other, taking breaks only for iced tea and cherry Popsicles.

"That will certainly be an asset." Granddad grins. "I'll have Connor come over Monday morning to discuss how the two of you will divide the work."

"Connor?" I echo stupidly. I don't see the net until it's fallen neatly around me.

"It's one of his projects for the summer, but I think he'd appreciate the help." Granddad looks downright *delighted*. If I didn't know better, between this and last week's lunch, I'd suspect he was playing matchmaker.

He probably just wants Connor to inspire me to greatness.

This means Connor will be here. In my house. A couple times a week.

I blush, irrationally worried that Granddad can see the lustful thoughts written across my face. "I… Uh, I…"

Granddad puts his hand on my shoulder. "That's not a problem, is it? I know you two didn't exactly hit it off last week, but—"

"No! Nope. Not a problem." I look up at the portrait of Dorothea. Even in death, she manages to stir up trouble. Bet she'd get a kick out of that.

"Good." Granddad practically claps. "I'll give him a call and ask him to come here Monday morning instead of going to the office. Ten o'clock okay? That should give you time to get to the pool first."

Trust him to notice, even in the midst of all this family drama, that I have been slacking on my training. He's right though. I don't want Charlotte Wu sneaking past me in the one-hundred-meter freestyle. "Yeah, that's perfect. I'm usually back by nine." That'll give me time to wash the chlorine out of my hair and maybe put on some makeup and—

It's not a date, Ivy. Keep it together!

"All right. You better get on to bed then."

"Okay. 'Night, Granddad. Love you."

As I head upstairs, padding barefoot past the closed

doors where my sisters and Erica sleep, my brain's conjuring up images of Connor and me. Working together. Sitting side by side on the buttery leather couch, hips and shoulders pressed together, heads bent as we puzzle out Dorothea's handwriting. I decipher a word, maybe say something clever, and Connor catches my hand. Holds it. Turns to me, his pretty, gold eyes full of admiration, and leans in and—

No way. Granddad will probably chaperone us the whole damn time.

But Granddad hates to run the central air, and even with the french doors open and the fan on, it gets stuffy in the library in the afternoons. He couldn't begrudge us a break. A swim, maybe. I picture Connor shucking off his shirt, and maybe his shorts too, standing on the dock wearing nothing but his blue-plaid boxers and his tattoos.

I groan and throw myself facedown on my bed.

What will I say when I see him? What will *he* say? Should I pretend nothing happened? Like he's just my…I don't know, my *coworker*? My coworker whom I daydream about seeing half-naked and making out with?

Oh no. What if he thinks I wheedled my way into this project as an excuse to see him again because I'm into him?

I've had a few hookups, a few kisses here and there, but I was never as into it as I was tonight with Connor. The boys were cute enough and nice enough and wanted to kiss me, so I let them. Two of them asked me out later, but I was too busy for a boyfriend—or so I told myself. I had swimming and studying and extra classes. I had Abby and Claire and Alex. That felt like enough.

But this is different. I *am* into Connor. And tonight it seemed like he was into me.

Was this a one-time thing, or could it be more?

CHAPTER

EIGHT

WHEN I GET BACK FROM THE POOL MONDAY MORNING, I EXPECT TO find Luisa sliding a pan of homemade cinnamon rolls into the oven, Granddad reading the *Cecil Gazette* at the table, and the kitchen filled with the scents of coffee and fresh-squeezed orange juice. I'll kick off my sneakers and throw my Cecil Warriors hoodie over the back of my chair, bend to hug Luisa, and complain that I'm starving after an hour in the pool. That's how we do mornings.

So it's a surprise when I throw open the back door and find Erica sitting at the kitchen table, her phone in one hand and a tall, slim glass of tomato juice in the other.

I'm tempted to walk right past her but I don't. I

can be mature about this. I can. I pull out my earbuds. "Good morning."

She looks up with a frown. "You're up early. Yesterday too."

I fight the urge to apologize. For everything. Being awake. Being in the kitchen. Being tall. Being born. We haven't spoken a single word to each other since that scene in the library. Other than the awkward family supper last night, where the conversation was carried mostly by Gracie and Granddad, I've managed to pretty well avoid her.

"I was at the pool," I explain. "I go most mornings. Free swim from seven till nine."

"Dedicated. Dad must love that." She makes a face. Her bottle-blond hair is a little less spiky today, but her eyes aren't. "When I was your age, you couldn't have pulled me out of bed before noon. Especially yesterday, after a bonfire party."

I shrug. "I wasn't out that late." I peer into the fridge. Luisa's been here after all, judging by the pitcher of orange juice. I wonder if she saw Erica and fled. I wouldn't blame her. "Where's Luisa?"

"I told her I had breakfast covered." Erica's chuckle is low, with a raspy catch to it. She stirs her drink with a celery stick. "Ever had a Bloody Mary?"

"No." I pour a glass of juice.

"There's vodka in the cabinet, if you want to make that a screwdriver."

"No, thanks." I smile, uncomfortable. "I don't think Granddad would approve."

"Don't you ever do anything he'd disapprove of?" She gazes at me over the rim of her glass. "I bet you don't. Jesus. How are you my kid?"

Is she *drunk*? I peer at her closely, but I don't know her well enough to tell. Still, it's the first time she's acknowledged that I'm her daughter. "Careful. You wouldn't want anyone to overhear that."

She waves a skinny hand laden with chunky silver rings. I think she *is* drunk. *Wow. It's only nine o'clock in the morning.*

"Nah. Grace is watching cartoons in the living room with Dad, and Iz won't be up for ages yet. She's like me. Likes her sleep. I can't sleep in this house though." She turns back to me. "I can't believe Dad lets you go to parties at the cove. Are they still fun?"

"It was fine." I lean against the counter, wary of her sudden interest.

"*Fine?*" she mimics. "That's it? Are you dating the housekeeper's kid?"

"No." I am careful to keep my voice even. Just thinking of Alex makes my heart hurt. He's never been that angry with me before. "Alex and I are just friends."

"Too bad. He's cute. And he's obviously got a thing for

you. Are you seeing somebody else?" She takes a bite of her celery stick.

I shake my head, pushing away thoughts of Connor. I am not about to confide in her about him. Or anything else. Mother or not, I don't trust her and I am not up for her drunk attempt at bonding. "No."

"Let me guess. You're too busy for a boyfriend. How many classes does Dad have you taking this summer? Ballet? French? Painting? Piano? Voice?" She stands up. In bare feet, she's a few inches shorter than me. "*Shit*. Can you sing?"

"No. Not well." I can't tell whether she's relieved or disappointed to find that we don't have that in common. Honestly, I couldn't carry a tune in a bucket. I tried out for chorus in seventh grade with Abby, and I still remember—vividly, viscerally—when we walked up to Mr. Kerns's door to check the list. Abby squealed when she saw her name, but mine wasn't there. Before that, I always sang confidently in the car, in the shower, around the house, assuming I'd inherited a little of my mother's talent. After that, I'd stopped.

If you're not any good, what's the point?

Milbourn girls don't do mediocre.

"Do you still sing?" I ask, curious despite myself.

"No. Not for years." Erica evades my eyes and takes a long sip of her Bloody Mary. Everyone says she had a gorgeous voice. Erica even admitted that she was happy singing with her band and waitressing. Why did she quit? And what does that do to a person? Giving up the thing you love most, stifling your talent. Is that why she's so unhappy? Does it poison you, slow and sure?

"You didn't answer me," she points out. "What classes are you taking this summer?"

"None." But I have taken all those classes at one time or another. This conversation is so strange. I don't know Erica at all, but she knows bits and pieces of my life. She lived them twenty years ago. "I'm volunteering at the library in town. And swimming."

"That's it? He's letting you slack off." The celery stick crunches as she bites off another piece.

I shrug, weirdly stung. Is he? Does he expect less from me than he did from her? "I hang out with my friends. Play Scrabble with Granddad. I read."

"You're such a little nerd." She says it almost affection-ately, but the way she's looking at me, scanning me from head to toe, is like she's trying to see straight through my skin. It's a little creepy, especially coming from someone who hasn't shown the slightest bit of interest in me for fifteen years. "I don't see myself in you at all."

Neither do I.

I've been searching for a resemblance in sly little moments at supper or passing her in the hall. Studying her when her head's turned.

I haven't found any similarities.

Not being like her is a *good* thing. That's what I've been told my whole life. So why does her saying that she doesn't see herself in me hurt so damn much?

"Good," I mutter, sliding the pitcher back into the fridge. I should go upstairs. Connor will be here in less than an hour and—

My mother grabs my arm. Spins me around so fast my hip smacks into the counter and I almost tumble off balance. She's sneaky without those heels.

"What did you say?" Her breath smells like tomato juice and nail polish remover.

I feel a second of guilt, but only a second. The urge to hurt her back is stronger. "I said, *good*. I've heard about you my whole life. What a screwup you were. What a slut. And selfish. How you didn't care about anybody but yourself. So far you've proven them all right."

She takes a step back. "You little bitch."

I'm so mad that I'm shaking. "I'd rather be a bitch than a pathetic drunk. Maybe instead of worrying about your ex finding out about me, you should worry that he'll find out you're drinking at nine a.m."

"Shut up." Her eyes narrow as she steps forward, her sharp chin jutting out. For a minute I think she might hit me and I shrink back against the counter.

"Stay out of this, Ivy," she says, seething. "I'm not

playing around. I don't care what you've heard. I'm a good mother to Grace."

"Yeah, well." I pick up my orange juice and walk past her. "I wouldn't know anything about that, would I?"

· · · · ·

In the bathroom, I turn up the music on my phone, blasting it, not caring if I wake up Isobel. This is *my* house. She can go complain to her mother.

There are unfamiliar products in my shower right next to my Hello Hydration shampoo and Yes to Coconut body scrub: brightly colored kids' shampoo, color-protection conditioner, and a body wash for oily skin. When I get out of the shower, both of my fluffy cornflower-blue towels are already damp. I frown, dripping water across the tiled floor as I rummage in the linen closet. Abby would laugh at me for being a spoiled only child, getting mad over a towel, but this is all I've ever known and those towels are *mine*. I wrap myself in an old, faded pink one and march upstairs to my room.

After I get dressed and braid my hair, there's still half an hour before Connor's due. I settle in with my laptop and pull up the college's website, specifically the summer course listings in the foreign language department. Summer classes started two weeks ago, but I bet Granddad could still get me in to audit. I'm already fluent in Spanish; Luisa's parents emigrated from Mexico and she helped me with my accent. Adding another language will look good on my transcripts though, and my middle-school summer-camp French is getting rusty.

There's an intermediate French class that's only one night a week. I can make time for that. I write the course number down on a sticky note to ask Granddad about later. Maybe he doesn't push me as hard as he did Erica because he's afraid I'll break, the way she did. But I won't. I'm stronger than that. I'll show them both that no matter what this summer throws at me, I can take it.

I take a deep breath and head downstairs, feeling somehow fortified.

Isobel has joined Erica in the kitchen. She's wearing black yoga pants and a baggy T-shirt and staring into a bowl that contains half a grapefruit. They stop talking when I walk in, and I'm left feeling like the one who doesn't belong here.

"Morning, Isobel." I grab a jar of peanut butter and a spoon and then lean against the counter, peeling a banana.

"Peanut butter is really fattening," Isobel informs me, tightening her messy ponytail. "And there are twice as many calories in a banana as in a grapefruit."

"Peanut butter also has a lot of protein," I say, since apparently we are exchanging nutritional data. "Which is great, because I just swam for an hour."

"Does swimming burn a lot of calories?" she asks.

"Yeah. But that's not why I do it." When I'm in the water, I'm all motion—breath and stroke and kick and turn. I'm pushing my body; I'm concentrating on what I can make it do, not how it looks. "I swim laps up at the college most mornings. We have a membership to the pool and the gym, if you ever want to join me." I glance nervously at Erica, hoping this won't set her off like Granddad's offer to teach Gracie how to swim.

Isobel fiddles with her spoon. "No way. I am not exercising in front of people. Or wearing a bathing suit. Mama and I are going to go for a run. Right, Mama?"

Erica gives her an absentminded smile before turning back to her phone. "Right."

"Ivy!" Granddad hollers from the hallway. "Connor's here!"

My stomach twists. Granddad must have seen him from the living room window. Connor didn't even have a chance to ring the doorbell. I was kind of hoping we might have a minute alone first.

"Who's Connor?" Isobel asks. Erica listens, head cocked like Abby's sisters' parakeet.

"One of Granddad's students. He and I are going to be working together on a project this summer." I am immediately conscious that I've called Granddad "Granddad" and not "Dad"—but maybe that's not weird, since he is Isobel's granddad? Gah, this is so unnecessarily complicated.

Erica glances up. "Letting Dad pick out your boyfriends?"

"It's not like that." I fight to keep from flushing.

"Sure it's not." She rolls her eyes.

It's too bad they don't get stuck at the back of her head so everybody could see that she's part demon. But I flee down the hall without arguing. I can take the high road.

Connor's standing just inside the front door. He's carrying a red computer bag and a tray of coffees from Java Jim. "I brought iced coffee," he says. "Black with three sugars for you, Professor. Ivy, this one's just black—figured you could doctor it however you want. Sorry, I—" He looks at me and I am caught like a butterfly pinned to a board. "I didn't know what you like."

My mind floods with extremely inappropriate responses.

"Uh, that's okay. Iced coffee's great. I… I'll go get some sugar," I say, taking the cup he's holding out. My fingers brush against his and I blush.

Granddad chuckles. "She's being polite. Ivy hates coffee."

I shoot him a murderous look. "Well, I was *trying* to be polite."

"You don't have to do that." Connor frowns. "What do you like? So I'll know for next time."

Next time. Like this is going to be a regular thing, him showing him up at my house with beverages.

For work. This is work, Ivy, not a date. I have to get my head together or I am going to make a fool of myself. I force myself to look at Connor like I am not torn between simultaneous urges to either hide or attack him in a fit of lust.

"Iced tea. Earl Grey, if they have it. One sugar. Thank you."

Connor shrugs. "It's no big deal. Employee discount."

Java Jim's opens at six a.m., so either Connor cut short a busy Monday morning shift to come over here, or else he swung by special to get us coffee. Either way, he's trying to impress someone.

The question is, is it me or Granddad?

Granddad leads us into the library, pontificating about Dorothea's journals and her dedication to writing in them every morning. How they're a mix of personal information—including some fairly salacious details about her crumbling marriage and her affair with Robert Moudowney—and notes on her works in progress. Occasionally there will be a scribbled rough draft of a poem, with lines that don't work crossed out and new phrases written in the margins. It's fascinating to be able to trace her thoughts and inspirations clearly.

Granddad used to buy me a journal every Christmas. I'd fill the first five or ten pages, writing diligently every night before bed, until I'd forget about it one night and quit. Last year at an end-of-semester barbecue, Granddad bragged to someone about my dedicated journaling. How I was just like Dorothea. I waited till the car ride home to set him straight, but from the look on his face, he was disappointed. Again.

"What an incredible resource." Connor runs his hand gently over the spines, and I remember him tracing *my* spine with the same careful attention. "May I?" he asks, setting the tray of coffee down on the desk.

"Of course. But no food or drinks anywhere near them." Granddad gives me a pointed look. "These are very valuable documents."

He talks about them—about everything of Dorothea's—like they belong in a museum. "It was the teeny, tiniest splotch of iced tea. You can still read everything!" I protest.

Connor selects a journal from the middle of the shelf and opens it, flipping pages reverently, squinting as he tries to decipher Dorothea's faded, spidery handwriting. "This is so cool." He looks up at Granddad. "Thank you. Thank you for trusting me with these."

"I know they're in good hands with you," Granddad says, and he does not add *unlike with my careless granddaughter, who once had the audacity to splash a drop of iced tea on these hallowed pages*, but he might as well have.

I sigh. "I'll be *really careful* this time, okay?"

"You better. I know some graduate students who would kill for this opportunity."

"Yeah, but you'd have to pay them more," I joke.

"Brat." Granddad laughs as he claps Connor on the shoulder. "I'm counting on you to keep an eye on her, Connor."

"I will, sir." Connor's face is inscrutable. Like he didn't have more than his eyes on me Saturday night.

"All right then. I'll leave the two of you to figure out how you'll divide the work. Ivy's very good at reading Dorothea's handwriting. It can take some getting used to, but I'm sure you'll manage." Granddad gives Connor an encouraging smile. "If you need anything, I'll be in the living room with Grace."

"We'll be fine," I promise.

We're quiet as he leaves. I can hear the jingle of some cartoon from the other room. I crouch and pick up the first journal, the one from 1942 when Dorothea was only sixteen. Her mother and little sisters had just been killed, and her father was off fighting in the Pacific. She was terrified that Robert Moudowney was going to drop out of school and enlist, and a year later he did. He lied about his age to join the marines and was wounded at Iwo Jima. It's all detailed in the next two journals.

When I stand, I meet Connor's gaze.

"Hey," he says.

"Hi." I offer a shy smile.

"Did you really do that? Spill iced tea on one of the journals?" he asks.

I sigh. "Granddad is never going to let me live that down. I was *fourteen*. I swear to God, I'll be super careful this time."

"He's right, you know. He could hire grad students." Connor stares at the journal in his hand like it could grow fangs and bite him.

"Yeah, but he'd have to import them from someplace else. We're right here, and we're cheap labor." I plop down in Granddad's leather recliner and cross my legs. "It's a good deal for him."

Connor's eyes land on my legs, but only for a second. "It's a good deal for *me*." For a second, my heart soars like a seagull because I hope he means working with me, but then he continues: "After I graduate, I want to get my MFA in poetry. This is the kind of thing that could really set me apart from other applicants." He takes a breath, running his hand over the back of his neck. He's nervous.

And it's not about being in the same room as me.

My heart drops like a wounded bird.

It wasn't me he was trying to impress with the coffee.

Connor puts the journal back before picking up his iced coffee and taking a sip. He leans against the desk. "This job is really important to me, Ivy. I don't want to screw it up."

I glance over my shoulder, making sure we're still alone. "Screw it up how? By making out with your professor's granddaughter?"

Connor's pretty eyes go wide. "No. Well, uh…maybe." His gaze drops to the floor. "I had an incredible time the other night, but—"

The "but" arrows into my heart, already sore from this morning's skirmish with Erica and Saturday night's battle with Alex.

"I understand," I interrupt breezily. I might as well be the one to say it. "It was fun and all—" I just about choke on the words but force myself to keep going, my voice a shade too loud. "I mean, I don't *regret* what happened—but it's probably not a good idea for it to happen again. Especially if we're going to be working together all summer. Things are pretty complicated for me right now anyway."

"Complicated. Right." Connor frowns.

"Right. So…" I glance over my shoulder again, then hop up, stroll closer—but not too close—and lower my voice. "If we're going to be working here, you should probably know that my mother hasn't told Gracie and Isobel that I'm their half sister. They think I'm their aunt."

"She told them the Professor is your father?"

I shrug. "In a lot of ways, he is. He raised me."

"And you agreed to this? You're just—going along with it?" I guess maybe I've given him the impression that I'm a pretty forthright girl, not the kind to mince words or tell lies and half-truths—except, of course, the one I'm telling right now, about how it would be better if we don't ever kiss each other again.

That is *such* a lie.

I find myself staring at his lower lip. Recall nibbling on it a little. I shrug again and paste on a smile. "Well, I wasn't given much of a choice. That's kind of how it goes around here."

But that's not true, is it? I could have pitched a fit when Granddad first told me Erica and the girls were coming. After they arrived, I could have been honest with him about how hard it would be having my mother in the same house, how much the things Erica's said have hurt me. I could have said no to working with Connor. Just now, I could have told Connor I want to see him again—not as his professor's granddaughter, but as me. Ivy.

"You have choices." Connor takes a deep breath. "If it makes you uncomfortable, me being here, us working together—"

Is he being chivalrous and offering to quit? "No," I interrupt. "This job is important to you. It'll be fine. No worries. Besides, Granddad would never let you quit without a damned good reason. He can't shut up about how great you are. It's sort of obnoxious, honestly."

"Really?" Connor looks delighted.

"Really."

"That means a lot. This is such an incredible opportunity for me. Seeing where one of my favorite poets lived, reading all about her life—I can't believe you grew up here."

He turns in a slow circle, examining Dorothea's old blue Smith-Corona typewriter, perched on the desk behind him; the bookcase full of her signed first editions and foreign editions; the portrait of her above the fireplace. "I know you said poetry isn't your thing, so maybe it's no big deal to you, but my mom's a payroll manager. My dad's an accountant. They met in business school. They don't get poetry. It's, like, *frivolous* to them. And my sister's just like them. A total math genius. I'm the anomaly."

"I know how it feels not to fit in," I say with a crooked, bittersweet smile.

What I don't say is that at least Connor has a normal family. Two parents still married to each other. A sibling he got to grow up with.

No one is expecting him to be extraordinary.

Except...I think he expects it of himself. I watch as he leans down, tripping his fingers lightly over those spines again, and he is so goddamn gorgeous I want to cry. He knows what he wants and he's going to make it happen. Part of me is crazy jealous of that. And the other part of me is crazy attracted to it—that passion, that ambition. It makes me want him more than I've ever wanted anyone.

Even though that ambition is what's standing in the way of him wanting me back.

CHAPTER
NINE

"AND THEN I CALLED MY MOTHER A SLUT," I EXPLAIN.

"Ivy! Don't use that word," Claire says, reaching around to tighten the knot on her black halter top. "It shames women for their sexual agency and reduces them to nothing but—"

"We *know*," Abby interrupts impatiently. She and I finished our Tuesday morning shift at the library an hour ago. She helped with preschool story time, and I shelved a whole cart full of books. Now we're at Abby's house, surrounded by paintings of Thomas Kinkade's cozy cottages, family portraits taken down by the water, washable slipcovers, muddy soccer cleats, and dog hair from their ancient cocker spaniel, Sunshine. I love Abby's house.

"I want to hear more about what happened with Alex. Have you talked to him since the party?" Abby is sprawled in the middle of the living room floor, petting Sunshine.

"Forget Alex." Claire is curled up on the green-flowered couch. "He was such a dick to her the other night."

"Because he's in love with her!" Abby defends.

"That doesn't make it okay." Claire grabs a handful of pretzel sticks from the bag on the coffee table. "Has he apologized to you, Ivy?"

"I haven't seen him," I admit. Usually Alex pops in and out of the kitchen while Luisa's cooking or comes over to go for a swim after he gets off work at the garden center. Or we pass each other coming and going in the driveway or while he's mowing the lawn. He must be avoiding me.

"Three days without talking is a long time for you two," Abby says.

She's right. It's not like us.

Only I'm not sure what *us* means anymore. If he can't be my boyfriend, does Alex still want to be my friend? The thought of losing him makes me want to cry. Usually he and Luisa come over for Sunday supper, but with Erica and the girls here, everything's different now. This Sunday, Luisa made a roast chicken with potatoes and squash and zucchini and then went back to the carriage house. Supper was brief and awkward, with Granddad and Gracie doing most of the talking while Erica drank half a bottle of white wine and Isobel picked at her vegetables.

What if things never go back to normal?

"Tell us more about your conversation with Connor," Claire says. "Why did you let him off the hook like that? It's okay to go after what you want. You don't have to play hard to get."

Abby scrunches her freckled forehead. "Maybe she doesn't want Connor."

"No, I do. But it's probably for the best."

I grab my glass of iced tea as Abby and Claire exchange deeply dubious glances. Claire and I have been friends since we were toddlers. The English department and the history department are in the same building on campus, and her mom brought Claire to the office one afternoon when I was there with Granddad. We bonded over Granddad's admin assistant's special stash of lollipops. Our duo became a trio after Abby and I sat next to each other in fifth grade homeroom and we geeked out over comic books together. Granddad is kind of a genre snob, so I started borrowing from Abby's amazing collection of graphic novels. We've been friends so long that Abby and Claire know when I'm lying. Or evading. Or trying to convince myself of something.

They are still watching me. Waiting for a real answer.

"Connor and I are going to be working together all summer," I continue. "It's too complicated. You know Granddad. He's protective."

"Patriarchal," Claire says darkly. "Your body is not—"

"We know!" Abby interrupts, and Sunshine barks, startled.

"You could quit the job," Claire suggests. "You can read Dorothea's journals anytime. It's not like you need the money."

"Must be nice," Abby says. She waitresses at the Crab Claw to save up for college, not because it looks good on a transcript. Her dad is a salesman down at the Ford dealership, her mom works part-time as a real estate agent, and with four kids, they have to stretch to make ends meet. Meanwhile, Claire's parents are both professors, and Granddad and I are pretty well off between his salary and Dorothea's estate. If I do end up staying in Cecil, my tuition will be free. That's another reason that the prospect of leaving, of considering other colleges, makes me feel like an ungrateful brat.

"Why would she quit a job she likes for a boy she barely knows?" Abby scratches Sunshine's ears to the rhythmic thump of the dog's tail against the floor. "Aren't you supposed to be the feminist here, Claire? Connor didn't even *protest* when Ivy said they shouldn't see each other again. She shouldn't have to compete with her granddad and her dead great-grandmother for a guy's attention."

Jesus. Abby has a point, but...

"Alex, on the other hand, is totally devoted to her."

"Stop pushing for her to get with Alex! She doesn't want to be with Alex," Claire says. "Besides, remember how he acted with Ginny West? Would you want him telling the whole baseball team about your sex life? Those guys are gross."

Abby toys with her infinity necklace. "Not all the guys on the team are like that. Ty isn't. And besides, Alex would never be like that with *Ivy*."

I take a deep breath. Count to ten. Remind myself that my friends love me and want what's best for me. "Could you two stop fighting, please? I've made up my mind, and I am not dating Alex *or* Connor. I'm going to work on this project and try to improve my butterfly and take a French class on Thursday nights—and try not to murder my mother. That's it. That's my summer."

Claire leans forward. "Wait. What French class?"

"Ivy!" Abby groans. "No classes. You promised."

"Wait," Claire says. "Did you literally get stressed out because of your mom and sign up for a college course?"

I stuff two pretzel sticks in my mouth so I can't answer. They both just stare at me till I finish chewing. "Uh, maybe? I like languages. I'm good at languages."

"You're good at lots of things," Abby says, ever loyal.

"Not good enough." I can't keep the bitterness from my voice.

Claire waves her pretzel stick at me threateningly. "Do not even start with that."

Mrs. Morris comes in, carrying a plate of freshly baked chocolate-chip cookies. "Girls? The cookies are ready! Want some?"

"Um, *yes*," Claire says, and I nod as Mrs. Morris puts the plate down on the coffee table next to our iced teas. I love that she doesn't worry about crumbs or calories or using coasters.

"Thanks, Mama," Abby says.

"Don't tell Luisa," I whisper, "but your chocolate-chip cookies are my favorite."

"It'll be our secret." Mrs. Morris smiles. Her straight, reddish-blond hair is pulled back into a ponytail, with little wisps escaping around her apple-cheeked face. She's short, like Abby, but plump. And she loves her kids so much. She's always in the stands cheering at the twins' soccer matches, and she's always in the front row with a bouquet of yellow roses—Abby's favorites—during chorus concerts. She even cut her hours back to part-time last year when Eli started having trouble in school.

I cannot imagine *any* situation in which she'd call Abby a little bitch.

Eli zooms through the doorway and across the floor on his Heelys, his shaggy, shoulder-length red hair flying out behind him. "Where are the cookies?"

"There are more in the oven for you," Mrs. Morris assures him.

Eli grabs two cookies off the tray and stuffs one in his mouth.

"Elijah! Be a gentleman! We have guests."

"It's just Claire and Ivy. They aren't real guests." Eli scowls and spins, his pink skirt flaring out, while Claire and I laugh. "And I told you to call me Ella! And I don't want to be a gentleman. They don't get to wear dresses. Ladies wear dresses. And princesses. I want to be a princess."

"Honey, we've talked about this." Mrs. Morris's face flushes. "It's okay to want to wear dresses and be a princess. It's okay to want to play with makeup and dolls. That doesn't mean you have to be a girl."

I glance at Abby, who is literally squirming, her eyes trained on the floor.

"But I told you, Mama, I *am* a girl," Eli says, and zooms off again.

Mrs. Morris starts after him, then pauses in the doorway. "I'm sorry. This is very confusing for all of us."

There's an awkward silence in Eli—Ella's—wake.

"How is he doing?" I ask tentatively.

Claire snatches a chocolate-chip cookie. "*She.*"

"He's a boy," Abby insists, her shoulders stiffening. "You heard Mama. Eli likes girl things, but he's still a boy. His therapist calls it gender-variant."

Claire shrugs. "I don't know, Abby. Sounds to me like she's transgender."

Oh Jesus. Cecil might be a college town, but the Eastern Shore is conservative, and a transgender six-year-old is not something most people are going to accept without any ugliness. I understand why Abby worries about Eli—Ella's— safety. About her being bullied.

"He's six!" Abby protests. "How can he know?"

"How do *you* know you're a girl?" Claire asks.

"What?" Abby looks at Claire like she's crazy. "It's not the same. I was born this way. I've got girl parts."

"God, Abby, you can say *vagina*," Claire says. "It's not a bad word."

Abby winces. I ignore them, thinking about Ella. I mean, if she wants to be called Ella, I should call her that, right? She says she's a girl, so we should treat her like one. Besides the pronouns, it's not really any different from how I treat her now. She's always liked wearing girls' clothes and playing with the twins' dolls. When she was a toddler, the Morrises thought it was cute, her wanting to be like her big sisters. She's only two years younger than the twins, and Mr. and Mrs. Morris thought maybe she felt left out.

But when she started kindergarten last year, they cut her hair short and told her she couldn't wear dresses outside the house—and Ella started acting out. Trying to hurt herself even. At the recommendation of her therapist, her parents started compromising: letting her grow out her hair and wear nail polish. But identifying as a girl is pretty new. I can see how it would take Abby's family some time to wrap their minds around it.

"Mama's taking him to that therapist once a week now," Abby says softly. "And Daddy's taking him fishing and to T-ball practice. It's been hard. On everybody."

"Imagine how hard it is on her. All the fishing and T-ball in the world isn't going to make her a boy," Claire says. "I bet she could really use her big sister's support."

"She is a boy. *He.*" Abby jumps to her feet. "I'm sorry, I've got to go see if Mama's all right. I'll catch you at the library on Thursday, Ivy."

"Abby—" I start, standing up.

"I'm fine," she says, blinking back tears. "I just want to check on Mama. She and Daddy have been fighting a lot this week. About Eli. *Ella.* God, I don't know. Daddy gets upset when any of us say Ella or call her 'she.' So I know you mean well, Claire, but I can't do this right now. Just—see yourselves out. Take some cookies."

She rushes out of the room. It's hard to imagine Mr. and Mrs. Morris fighting. They still hold hands in public.

"Stop looking at me like that," Claire says.

"You need to give them a little time. They'll come around. Even Mr. Morris, I bet."

"I hope so. This town is so backward. People barely understand what bisexual means. Transgender is going to be a real stretch. There's a reason more kids aren't out at school. Do you know how many times I got told I was going to hell this morning walking into the clinic?"

"Is that why you're so grumpy?" I take a chocolate-chip cookie. It's still warm and gooey and streaks my hand with chocolate.

"Might have something to do with it." Claire sighs. "It sucks having to walk through that crowd of crazies. There was a girl our age who came into the clinic with her aunt to get tested for STDs, and she was already scared and embarrassed. It's her body. It's nobody else's business what she was there for."

"I agree," I say, "but the Morrises are good people. They'll figure this out. They love each other. Ella will be okay."

Claire stands up, stretching her arms above her head, coming dangerously close to flashing me as her yellow skirt lifts to her upper thighs. She fixes me with an unsettling look of pity. "Ivy, for a smart girl, you are super, super naive sometimes."

·····

Back home, I'm relieved that Erica's car isn't in the driveway. I let myself in through the back door and find Granddad, Gracie, and Isobel at the table. Granddad and Gracie are eating bowls of cherry cobbler with scoops of vanilla ice cream. Isobel is having a bowl of cherries and a Diet Coke and scowling. Childishly, I wonder if her face will get stuck that way. The kitchen smells heavenly: brown sugar and tart cherry and sweet vanilla. For the first time in days, I am glad to be home.

"Aunt Ivy!" Gracie lost one of her front teeth last night and is even more adorable now, if that's possible.

"Hey, you! Did the tooth fairy come visit you last night?" I ask.

She nods and pulls a wrinkled dollar bill from her pocket. She stretches it out for me to admire. "Mama said I can spend it on anything I want! She said she'll take me in town to get candy later this week. Said maybe we could get milk shakes too."

I sit in the empty chair between her and Isobel. "Mr. Jacobs makes the best milk shakes in town. The strawberry ones are my favorite."

"Me too! Strawberry milk shakes are my favorite too." Gracie seems delighted whenever we have anything in common, from favorite superheroes (Black Widow) to favorite vegetables (broccoli). "Iz likes chocolate."

"Well, Iz isn't going to get one because milk shakes

are a million goddamn calories and she's a cow," Isobel snaps.

"Isobel," Granddad says, tapping his spoon against the side of the bowl. "Language."

"What? Mama doesn't care if I cuss," Iz protests.

"Well, I do, and this is my house. I want you girls to feel at home here, but there are a few rules you need to follow, and not cussing—especially in front of your little sister—is one of them," Granddad says. "Also, you are not a cow. You're a lovely young lady."

"Whatever." Isobel rolls her eyes. Today they're rimmed in thick blue liner. "This place sucks and I'm too old to be bribed with a milk shake. I want to go home."

Gracie looks back and forth between Granddad and me and Isobel. "I miss Daddy, but I like it here," she says, ever the little peacemaker. Her hair is arranged in two long braids, and I wonder who did them for her—Isobel or Erica? I can't imagine my mother having the patience to braid her little girl's hair, but maybe she did. For Gracie's sake, I hope she did.

"I'm glad." Granddad gazes at Isobel as he eats another spoonful of cobbler. "I know this is difficult for you, Isobel. What were your original plans for your summer? Gracie mentioned some kind of drama camp."

"Musical theater camp," Isobel corrects, rocking back on her chair legs. "I've gone the past three summers. We get to work with professional directors and choreographers, and at the end of July we were going to put on a production of *Legally Blonde*."

Granddad picks up a stack of papers on the table. "I know it's not the same, but we do have a theater camp here. It starts next week. Looks like they're doing *Peter Pan* this year."

"*Peter Pan!*" Gracie squeals. "You should do it, Iz. That sounds so fun. Maybe you could be Tinkerbell."

Isobel glares. "Then *you* do it."

"Well, it's for ages eight to fifteen, so Grace is still a little young." Granddad flips through the stack of brochures and flyers. "If you don't think that would be a good fit, there are other options for us to look at. Gracie, what about you? The Arts League offers some half-day camps for kids your age. There's language play—that's like storytelling—and sculpture and drawing and eco-art..."

Claire was right; I am naive. Because I didn't see this coming and I should have. I thought Granddad was trying to help Isobel, to give her a reason to get out of the house and make friends instead of moping around. And that may be part of it, but there's another agenda here too: Granddad's desire to extend the Milbourn family legacy.

"I like to draw," Gracie says, and I can almost hear Granddad's heart go pitter-pat. Another artist in the family!

"Do you now?" he asks, and Gracie nods, her blond

braids bouncing. "There are all kinds of classes. It doesn't have to be art. There are ballet and gymnastics and—"

"I like drawing best," Gracie insists. "I want to learn how to swim like Aunt Ivy too, but Mama says I can't. So maybe gymnastics would be fun. I can already do a cartwheel. Wanna see?" She jumps up from her chair.

"Why don't you show me later outside? No cartwheels in the house," Granddad says, but he is positively beaming. "We'll get you set with those two classes for now, and Isobel, you can do your theater camp, and—"

"I don't want to do your stupid small-town theater camp," Isobel snaps. "None of my friends will be there. *Kyle* won't be there."

"Kyle's her boyfriend," Gracie stage-whispers to Granddad.

"Well, no, your friends won't be there. But maybe you'll make new friends. It could still be fun," Granddad says.

"What's the point? It's not like I'm ever going to be a real actress. Look at me!" Isobel gestures to herself, the curves of her breasts, her stomach, her hips. "I'm a heifer."

"You are not! You're so pretty," I say. "You don't have to be a size zero to be pretty. You could totally be an actress."

Isobel slams down her Diet Coke. "And play what? The fat, funny best friend?"

"What about a different class then?" Granddad is not one to give up. "Do you play any instruments? Or what about voice lessons? That could help you with theater camp next summer. Or dance? Piano? Ivy's tried all of those. What was your favorite, Ivy?"

"Um…" All I can remember is the crushing realization in the first few days of each class that I had no natural aptitude for any of them. That none of them were my mythical Milbourn gift.

Iz stands up, shoving her chair back with a screech. "Look, I'm not a little kid. I don't want to take any of your stupid classes, okay?"

Granddad looks at her, bewildered. I've compromised. Negotiated. But I never once flat-out refused. "Then what will you *do* all summer?"

"I don't know. Watch TV? Text my friends? Wait for it to be September?"

Granddad scrubs a hand over his beard. "That's all?" He sounds horrified. The idea of a truly lazy summer is utterly foreign to him.

"That's my plan, yeah."

Much like Claire, sometimes Granddad just does not know when to stop. "I don't believe in wasting a whole summer like that, Isobel. You don't have to decide right this minute, but why don't you take a look at these flyers and see if there's something else that interests you?"

Isobel looks down at him, her brown eyes narrowed. She doesn't take the papers. "Do I have to? Is that one of your rules? Like, if I don't take a class, you'll kick me out?"

I hold my breath. I'm not sure which answer she's hoping for. Which answer *I'm* hoping for. Even Gracie is quiet.

"No," Granddad says. "Of course not. But I'd like you to consider it. Hopefully one of your mother's job applications will pan out and she'll be working soon. I'll be up at the college a few days a week. Ivy has two jobs and swimming, and if Gracie's at camp—"

"Don't worry about me. I can take care of myself." Isobel grabs another Diet Coke out of the fridge. "I'm used to it."

CHAPTER
TEN

CONNOR ARRIVES PROMPTLY AT TEN O'CLOCK THE NEXT MORNING TO work on Dorothea's journals. When he knocks on the door, I can't contain my smile. Granddad's up on campus, but Connor's brought an iced coffee for himself and an iced tea for me. "Nice shirt," he says, nodding to my blue *I Know I Swim Like a Girl—Try To Keep Up* tank top.

In the library, he carefully moves Dorothea's typewriter to the side and sets up his laptop. Since I'm already familiar with her handwriting, for now I'm dictating and he's typing. I curl up in Granddad's armchair, tucking my bare feet beneath me. I've always liked reading out loud. Back in elementary school when our teachers used to ask for volunteers, I was always Hermione, waving my hand wildly. Connor's ink-stained fingers fly over his keyboard. He seldom needs me to repeat myself, only asks me to spell out a few names, references to family or neighbors.

It's not until I hear his stomach growl that I glance up and realize it's almost one o'clock. I close the journal and set it aside. "Ready for a lunch break?"

"Yes. I'm starving," Connor says immediately.

"Me too. And crazy thirsty." My voice is getting a little husky. I stand and stretch.

"I could go home and come back in an hour, if that works for you."

I walk to the french doors and look out. Rain's been tapping steadily against the windows all morning. The Bay melts right into the misty sky. "You can stay if you want. We have leftovers. Roast chicken. I could throw together a salad."

"You sure?" Connor asks.

"I wouldn't offer otherwise," I reassure him.

But that's not true, is it? I say lots of things I don't mean, especially lately. I've always prided myself on being forth-right. Granddad raised me to speak up. But lately, it seems like when it really matters, I back off. Back down.

In the kitchen, I throw an empty wine bottle into the recycling bin. Load a sticky wineglass into the dishwasher. Then I notice that while I've been trying to erase any trace of Erica from the kitchen, Connor has been hovering.

"How can I help?" he asks.

I shake my head. "You're a guest. You don't have to help. Sit down."

He shrugs. "I don't mind. Grams took care of Ani and me a lot when we were kids, and she was big on us helping out around the house. Especially me. Said there was no reason a man couldn't learn to cook, and she wasn't going to let me be as useless as my grandfather."

I grin. "I like your grams."

He smiles as I hand him the cutting board and a knife. "She used to be a high school English teacher. She read to us all the time. And made sure we spoke properly. I got teased a lot when I was a kid for talking too white. But she's the only one in my family who gets poetry. Who gets *me*." My breath catches at the loss in his voice. I feel a rush of gratitude that, at sixty, Granddad is still sharp as a tack.

I turn on the radio, tuned to the oldies station that Granddad likes. Connor and I work side by side at the granite countertop, humming along to "Hey Jude." I cut up the roast chicken and slice a few hard-boiled eggs; he chops tomatoes and peppers and onions. I throw together a quick vinaigrette—Luisa doesn't believe in store-bought salad dressings—while he slices homemade bread. The only sounds are the rasp of his knife and the swish of my whisk and the patter of rain against the windows. It's cozy. Companionable.

Or it would be if I weren't hyperaware of his every move—the proximity of his hip to mine, his elbow to mine, the rise and fall of his breath. I find myself watching him out of the corner of my eyes, noting the steadiness of his hands. He smells like coffee again.

Does he notice when I lean over and my ponytail brushes his upper arm? Does he see the flush that spreads across my cheeks when I hand him the bread knife and our fingers touch? Is it totally obvious that I want to put down the kitchen utensils and push him up against the counter and kiss him senseless?

Why did I tell him that we shouldn't kiss each other again?

I hand him plates and silverware, and he sets the table while I mix the salad. We've barely sat down to eat when the back door flies open. There's a rush of rain and wind and—

Alex.

Alex stops just inside the door, his dark hair dripping. It reminds me of the night the power went out and I learned Erica was coming home. Was that only a week ago?

"I-I was just looking for Ma." His eyes dart from me to Connor and back again.

"It's Wednesday," I remind him.

"Right. I forgot," he says, and I wonder if this was just an excuse to come by the house. To see me. Apologize, maybe. His jaw tightens as he takes in Connor and me. I realize we are sitting closer than we need to, side by side instead of across from each other. "What's he doing here?"

"Working." I try to keep the annoyance from my voice, but it slips out. This is my house. I don't need his approval to have guests over.

"*Working?*" Alex doesn't try to keep the skepticism from his voice.

I grit my teeth. "Yes. We're transcribing Dorothea's journals so they can be archived online. We're taking a lunch break."

"You know what? Never mind. None of my business." He turns to go, and I leap out of my chair, suddenly, irrationally worried that if he disappears out into the rain I won't ever see him again.

"Wait, I—" I take a few steps forward. "Alex, can we talk?"

He hesitates in the doorway, then turns and walks past us, down the hall toward the library.

"Connor, I'll be right back. I'm sorry. I need…" I trail off, because how does that sentence end? I need to fix this? I don't know if that's possible. I need to apologize? I don't have anything to apologize for.

Alex is pacing in front of the french doors. "What do you want?" he asks without turning to face me. "I'm sorry for interrupting your date, okay?"

"It's not a date." I wish it were. But it's not. "Are you still mad at me?"

"No." He won't meet my eyes.

"Well, what are you then?" I tug on the sleeve of his T-shirt, and he jerks away as if my touch hurts him. As if *I* hurt him. Alex and I touch each other all the time. It doesn't mean anything. Except maybe it did—*does*. To him. My throat knots.

"I don't know what I am, Ivy. Not everybody wants to sit around and talk about poetry and *feelings* all the time, okay?" he snaps. "Maybe I am mad at you. Maybe I'm mad at myself for not listening when you told me no the first time. Maybe I want to punch that guy in the kitchen and it's taking a lot of my energy not to do that."

"This isn't about Connor," I say. "This is about us."

"There is no *us*," Alex says. "You made that pretty fucking clear."

I take a step back. We've had fights before, but not like this. "You're my friend. One of my best friends. That doesn't have to change."

He shakes his head. "You think your boyfriend will be okay with me coming over for movie night and putting my arm around you when you're scared? Giving you a massage when your shoulder hurts? What about helping you put on sunscreen? Holding your hand?"

I bite my lip. "He's not my boyfriend." But I know that's

missing the point. Those things were kind of boyfriend things. More-than-friend things anyhow. I guess I never thought about it that way before.

"You've been avoiding me. I haven't seen you for four days," I point out. "That's not like us. We have an argument, we talk about it. We work things out."

Alex's shoulders are rigid. "I don't know what *us* is anymore. I think I need some time."

"Time?" The knot in my throat twists. Why does it feel like we're breaking up? "How *much* time?"

"I don't know, okay?" Alex has never talked to me like this before, like everything I say is stupid and frustrating. "A while. I can't see you every day. I can't watch you making out with some other guy. I can't go swimming with you and hang out and have dinner here like I'm part of the family."

"But you are family," I whisper, my voice wobbly.

"I'm not." His brown eyes are angry. "I need some space, okay? Don't make a big deal out of it."

He storms out the french doors into the rainy backyard without waiting for a response and I'm left curling into myself, blinking back tears. "Okay."

I count to ten. Take deep breaths. Then I paste on a smile and walk back into the kitchen, more apologies at the ready. Connor is scribbling in a little Moleskine notebook. His handwriting is cramped and messy, slanted a little. He caps the pen and closes the notebook before sliding them into the pocket of his cargo shorts. "Is everything okay?"

I nod, sitting down and picking up my fork. "Great."

"Sorry if I caused another argument between you and your…friend."

The way he says *friend*, the hesitation, makes it clear what he thinks. I fiddle with my fork, remembering how I let Alex drag me away on Saturday night. How Connor's grin faded when Alex took my hand—when I *let* Alex take my hand, even though I'd been kissing Connor. And now I interrupted our lunch and left him alone in my kitchen so I could argue with Alex. What kind of message does that send?

"Alex and I are friends. We grew up together." I explain how he and Luisa moved in when my mother left. "He's family."

Connor shakes his head. "That guy isn't looking at you like you're his sister."

"Well, I'm not looking back," I say. "He wanted more. I told him no." I take a deep breath. "We had a pretty big fight Saturday. He had no right to act like that. He has no say in who I kiss."

"Yeah?" Connor's voice is quiet. His hand rests next to mine on the table. "You said things were complicated for you right now."

"With my mother," I clarify. "And my sisters who don't

know I'm their sister." I inch my hand a little bit to the left. "I-I thought maybe you were more interested in Granddad than me."

Connor laughs, and his hand covers mine. I like the weight of it. The way his fingers intertwine with mine. His eyes linger on me, and I lean in, and—

The front door bangs open. "Ivy? Connor?" Granddad calls. I love him more than anyone else in the world, but I could about murder him right now.

Connor sits back in his chair, and I do too, somehow knocking my fork off my plate. It clatters onto the floor. When Granddad comes into the kitchen, I am literally under the table.

"Taking a lunch break? That salad looks good. Is there enough left for one more?" he asks, as clueless as the day is long. He grabs silverware and a plate and pulls out a chair. "How's the work going?"

"Um, good," I say, crawling back into my seat.

Connor gives me a shy smile. "I think we're making some progress."

CHAPTER
ELEVEN

THE NEXT AFTERNOON, I DECIDE TO STOP BY JAVA JIM'S AFTER MY
shift at the library. Their black currant iced tea is pretty
good, but mostly I'm hoping to see Connor. After
Granddad showed up at lunch yesterday, Connor and
I didn't have another minute alone. Granddad kept
telling stories about Dorothea, and then he insisted on
bringing out an old family photo album. We looked
at pictures of Great-Great-Grandmother, posing next
to the roadster that she and two of her daughters
would be killed in; Dorothea, standing on the front
porch next to Robert Moudowney before he went off
to war; Grandmother, playing in the backyard with
thunderclouds in the distance.

Connor was a rapt audience, captivated by the Milbourn family archive. He seems more of a mind with Granddad when it comes to our legacy—that it's a gift, not a curse; that the Milbourn women were extraordinary, not doomed. But I look at my mother, at Isobel and Gracie, and I don't know. Will they be okay? Will I?

I really, really want to believe that it's *me* Connor wants and not just a Milbourn. He already has the job; he doesn't need to kiss me to get it.

When I texted with Claire, she asked, **Why is it so hard for you to accept that maybe he likes you?** I didn't know how to respond. I guess I feel like there must be some catch. Like being me isn't enough. In this town, I'm never just Ivy. It's Ivy *Milbourn*. Everything I do, everything I am, reflects back on my family.

But Connor smiled at me. He held my hand. He wanted to kiss me, I think.

I definitely wanted to kiss him.

It's probably not cool to want to define what's happening between us, but I do. And I know he's working at Java Jim's this afternoon.

I'm in no hurry to get home anyhow. Dinner last night was a disaster. I made gazpacho and served it with some of Luisa's homemade bread. It was lovely for about ten minutes, till Erica warned Isobel that the bread would go right to her hips. Iz stormed upstairs and slammed her door, and Gracie cried because Mama hurt Izzy's feelings. Then Granddad started railing about the damaging way Erica talks to Isobel, how she's going to encourage an eating disorder and doesn't she realize she's going to pass on her unhealthy relationship with food to her daughter, and also did she really need to drink half a bottle of wine with dinner?

While I did not disagree with Granddad's points, I thought the middle of supper was maybe not the best time to make them. I ended up hiding out in the kitchen with Gracie, eating the rest of the vanilla ice cream and watching funny YouTube videos of cats.

"I miss Daddy," Gracie said plaintively at one point, as Erica hollered at Granddad, and I wondered if maybe it would be better to have the truth come out then and there if it meant the girls would end up back with Gracie's dad.

It's not my choice to make, and I don't know how Erica was before she showed up on our doorstep, but she seems to be unraveling fast. She's been going out every afternoon, supposedly to fill out job applications, but she comes back hours later reeking of cigarettes and already a few drinks in. Granddad offered to talk to Robby Griffin down at the Cormorant about whether they could use another hostess, but Erica pitched a fit about him trying to run her life. I'm still waiting for the explosion when she finds out that he signed Gracie up for those gymnastics and drawing classes.

Mostly I just keep my mouth shut and feel like I'm being disloyal to everyone, including myself. Between Granddad and Erica's shouting matches, Isobel's scowls, and Alex's disappearing act, home isn't much fun anymore.

I pause in front of the picture window of the Book Addict, pretending I'm checking out their "If You Like *Game of Thrones*, Try This" display, but really I'm trying to see if Judy is at the register. The owner of the Book Addict is the biggest gossip in town. There is no way in hell she hasn't noticed that Erica's back, and I am not up for being poor-deared to death about it.

Her co-owner, Susan, sees me and waves me in. They're a funny pair. Judy's tall and loud, with a mop of brassy red hair and an endless supply of gauzy scarves. Susan's tiny, wispy, and whispery, with striking, almost waist-length white hair. She always dresses in all black, so when I was little I thought she was a tragic widow, till one morning I saw her over on Water Street watering her roses while her husband read the *Gazette* on their front porch.

"Ivy Milbourn!" Susan whisper-shouts as I walk in. "Judy, look who's here!"

I put on a smile and look to the back of the store.

It's worse than I'd imagined. Judy has my sisters cornered in the children's section.

I start panicking immediately. What are they doing here? What is my mother thinking, bringing them into town? I guess it's not realistic to keep them cooped up in the house all summer, but it's not realistic to try to keep this secret either. She should've thought of that before she lied.

Gracie is petting the Book Addict's fat tabby cat, Sir Toby. Isobel is slouching against a rack of Elephant & Piggie books.

"Ivy Milbourn!" Judy shrieks. "I was just telling your sisters about the concert in the square tomorrow night!"

I barely hear what she says after *your sisters* because my heart starts pounding so hard it echoes in my ears.

I told Erica this was a stupid plan. I told her the truth wouldn't stay secret. *I told her.*

But Isobel is looking at Judy like she's a bit dim, not like she's revealed a life-altering family secret. Maybe I can play this off like Judy misunderstood and assumed we were sisters since Iz and I are so close in age. Judy is mid-monologue about the bluegrass band scheduled to perform tomorrow night when I grab Gracie's elbow and start towing her toward the door.

"Sure, that sounds super fun. We'll bring a picnic," I lie. If we escape the bookshop, there is no way we are going to that concert. We'd be sitting ducks for Judy and all the other old gossips. "You like picnics, right, Gracie? There's a farmers market this afternoon. Let's go get some peaches to bring with us!"

"Sure," Gracie says, and Iz allows me to herd them

toward the door, though she rolls her eyes at my sudden enthusiasm for produce.

"Oh, that's a wonderful idea. Stan's got fresh cherries too," Judy says. We weave through the mystery section and are almost at the door when she adds: "It must be real nice for you to have your sisters home for the summer, Ivy."

Isobel stops short, giving me a disdainful look. "We're not her sisters."

Judy laughs. Laughs! Like Iz is trying to trick her. "Of course you are, honey. Half sisters, I guess—we never did hear who Ivy's daddy was—but Gracie looks just like your mama when she was little. And you—well, Erica used to sulk all around town too when she was your age." Judy turns back to me, utterly oblivious to how much I want to strangle her. "I always felt awful sorry for you, sweetheart, growing up in that big old house all alone. It's about time Erica came home and made amends for the way she ran off."

Isobel is staring at me now with those big, brown eyes rimmed in black eyeliner. I can never do eyeliner right. I rub my eyes and it smears or gets in my contacts, and then I'm left blinking and blind all day.

"I think you're confused," Iz says carefully to Judy. "Ivy's mama died when Ivy was just a baby."

Gracie nods. "That's how come Mama won't let me learn to swim, 'cause our grandma Grace drowned. Mama named me after her."

"That's right," I say loudly, glaring at Judy, daring her to contradict me.

Susan catches on and clears her throat. "Judy, come over here and look at this Ingram order for me, will you?"

"What order?" Judy asks. Susan gestures her over with wide, insistent eyes.

"What was she talking about, Ivy?" Isobel's voice is shrill. "She's confused, right?"

I'm silent. I can't—won't—lie. Not when she's asking me straight out. "I think we should go home."

But the answer is pretty obvious now, and Isobel's smart. "She's not confused at all, is she? Mama lied to us. *You* lied to us. Granddad lied to us, and—"

"I'm sorry." I keep my voice low. Susan is fiddling with some paperwork, but Judy is watching the drama unfold from behind the counter. "I hated keeping it from you."

"But you did. Everybody in this whole stupid town knows the truth, don't they? Everybody but Gracie and me."

"I really think we should go home. Erica ought to be the one to explain." I gesture to Grace, who looks bewildered. I am horribly conscious of Susan and Judy standing on the other side of the cash register, listening to every painful word.

I am embarrassed, and I am angry. So angry. Erica *should* have been the one to explain this. Weeks ago. Years ago.

Why did she have to keep me a secret?

"Why do you call her Erica when she's your mother?" Isobel asks. "Is that just in front of us? Like, for show?"

"I call her Erica because until last week I hadn't seen or spoken to her in fifteen years. We've never had any kind of a relationship." I lean down to Gracie. "But I am so glad—*so glad*—to get to meet you two. I've always wanted sisters."

"This is really fucked up," Isobel says, and I cannot disagree.

Gracie's eyes go wide. "Izzy said the f-word!"

"Sometimes when people get mad, they cuss. It's okay. She's not mad at you. Right, Iz?" Isobel has the right to be mad at everybody else, but Gracie is so little; this must be super confusing for her.

Isobel leans down and gives Gracie a quick, distracted hug. "No, 'course not."

"Let's go home, okay? We'll talk to Erica. She can explain why she—"

"She's not at home," Isobel says. "She's at that coffee shop."

She pushes out the door, and I stare after her for a minute before I realize what's happening.

"Wait. No. Isobel, please!" I chase her down the brick sidewalk. Gracie grabs my hand and runs with me.

Please don't let her make a scene.

Iz bursts into Java Jim's. Marches through the shop to the little courtyard out back, where Erica is having a

cigarette and an iced coffee. Half a dozen people are enjoying the afternoon sunshine at little wrought-iron tables.
Ginny West's mom is over by the fountain with Cooper
Sutton's mom, chatting over blueberry scones and iced tea.
My retired third-grade teacher, Mrs. Summers, is playing
chess with her husband. Charlotte Wu is here with Katie
Griffith, another one of the girls from swim team. Katie
waves at me but I don't wave back. I'm too busy scanning
the courtyard, hoping that Connor is on break or out sick
or something, *anything*, to keep him from witnessing this.

He's here. Clearing glasses from a table. He looks up and
sees me and smiles.

"You lied to us," Isobel accuses her mother. Loudly.

Erica glances from Isobel to me. She pushes her sunglasses
to the top of her head. "You little bitch. I told you to stay
out of this." Her voice is part furious and part admiring. As
if she can't believe I had the gumption to disobey her. As if
this is something *she* would do.

Maybe she's still looking for little pieces of herself in me.

I hope she never finds them.

"You've been lying to us *our whole lives*," Isobel continues. "That is really messed up."

Erica ignores Iz, her eyes locked on me. "I can't
believe you told them. I didn't think you had it in you."
Like wrecking my sisters' lives is something I would do.
Something I would relish.

Isobel steps between us, waving her arms to get her mother's attention. "It wasn't Ivy, okay? The lady in the bookstore told us. Did you really think we wouldn't find out? That you could bring us here and still keep it secret? Why would you *do* this?"

I glance around the courtyard. The Summerses have abandoned their chess game. Mrs. West is eating her scone and staring at us like she's at the movies. *Everyone* is staring—including Connor.

"Please," I whisper, slouching, "can we talk about this at home?"

Erica lifts her chin. Raises her voice. "Oh, I'm sorry, are we *embarrassing* you?"

She's so spiteful. So childish. But why am I surprised?

"They're not. You are," I snap. "But that's not new. I was embarrassed by you before I ever met you."

It's a mean thing to say, but I am past caring.

Grace is huddled close to the prickly pink rosebush, like she's trying to blend in. "I don't understand, Mama. Why did you tell us Aunt Ivy is our aunt and not our big sister?" Her voice is small.

Erica leans forward. "Because your daddy wants to take you away from me and keep you all to himself. If you lived with him, you wouldn't get to see Iz or me except for visits. If a judge heard about how I gave up Ivy—"

"You're lying. Dad wouldn't do that." Isobel folds her

arms across her chest. "He wouldn't separate Grace and me. He'd keep both of us."

"He doesn't have any right to you," Erica says. "He's not your father."

Gracie throws herself at Iz, knocking her back a step, wrapping her arms around her big sister's waist. "No! I don't want to go live with Daddy by myself. I would miss you too much!"

"I wish you weren't my mother," Isobel chokes out. "I hate you."

Erica glances at me like she's fully expecting me to say *I told you so.*

I think it, but I don't say it. Not out loud.

Erica gives Iz a glittering smile, sliding her sunglasses back into place. "Watch your mouth. Soon I might be all you've got."

"That's not true. That will *never* be true." I turn to Isobel and Gracie. "You have me. And Granddad. We're not the kind of people who leave."

"No," Erica says. "You're the kind of people who drive everyone away."

CHAPTER
TWELVE

THERE'S A PART OF ERICA THAT LOVES THIS, I THINK. MAKING A scene. Breaking things. Even if those things are her own daughters.

Still, I'm shocked that she aims her arrow so true. *You're the kind of people who drive everyone away.* Erica doesn't know me, but she's managed to zero in on my greatest fear: that I'm not enough, will never be enough, for anyone to love.

I have to get out of here. Now. I can't be in the same place as her another minute. Even outside, there's not enough air.

I run. I'm halfway down the block, past the Cormorant and the SunTrust, before Connor catches up to me.

"Ivy! Ivy, wait!" he calls.

"I can't. I have to go." I can't look at him. I don't want to see the pity on his face. I concentrate on my feet instead, on not tripping over the uneven brick sidewalk in my polka-dot flats.

"Let me at least walk you home."

I steal a glance. He's still wearing the brown Java Jim's apron. Did he just walk out in the middle of his shift?

"I'm not going home."

You're the kind of people who drive everyone away. It plays over and over in my head.

Granddad never talked about Erica much, and I figured that was because their estrangement was painful for him. As I grew up though, everyone else started to tell me stories about her. How she was selfish. Reckless. Troubled. Part of me wondered if they were trying to convince me that something broken in *her* made her leave, not something broken in *me*. But both must be true. She is awful, sure, but I am the reason she left. She hated me so much that she didn't tell my sisters I exist—even before Grace's custody was an issue. And seeing me again hasn't changed her mind one bit.

"Ivy." Connor grabs my hand and hauls me to a stop. "Where are you going?"

I study the roses in front of the post office, afraid that if I look at him, I'll start crying, and I can't—won't—cry in the middle of town. Although I don't know why I'm trying to save face. The scene back in the courtyard will be all over Cecil by suppertime. How could it not?

"I don't know."

"Do you want me to call your granddad?"

"No!" Granddad will find out soon enough, and then there will be more *I told you so*'s and more fights. Probably more wine and cigarettes and slammed doors. Right about now, I'd trade them for all the loneliness and unanswered questions of my childhood.

Iz and Gracie will never know a childhood without all the drama, I guess.

Or was Erica different—better—before?

I swallow hard. Maybe when I'm not around, my mother isn't a monster.

"My apartment's right over on Queen Street. Do you want to go there?"

I finally look up. There's concern in Connor's pretty brown eyes, but not pity. And his fingers are threaded through mine. "Don't you have to get back to work?"

He shakes his head. "My shift's almost over. I'll text Kat. She'll cover for me." He reaches over and tucks a wayward curl behind my ear, his fingers brushing against my neck. Even now, even when I am a complete mess, his touch sends tingles all the way down to my toes.

"Yeah." I take a deep breath, clutching his hand. "Okay."

Connor doesn't let go of my hand till we get to his place

and he has to fish in his pocket for keys. He's renting an old two-story house that's been divided into apartments, one upstairs and one down. Inside, there's a cluttered living room with an ugly, blue-plaid couch, some plastic crates that serve as end tables, and a big TV with an Xbox hooked up to it. Java Jim's coffee cups are scattered on every surface, and books are stacked knee-high along the front wall beneath the curtainless windows.

Connor shoves his keys into his pocket and starts picking up some of the empty cups. "Sorry it's kind of a mess."

"I don't care." I flop down on the couch, sinking deep into the cushions.

"Do you want to talk about what happened back there?" Connor asks. "I can leave you alone if you want. If you need some space. My roommate won't be home for a while. He works up at the college for the IT department."

"I don't need space." Not from him anyway.

He puts down the stack of coffee cups and sits on the other end of the couch, leaving a good two feet between us. "So. That was your mom, huh?"

I can't help it. I burst into tears.

"I'm sorry," I sob, burying my face in my hands. "I don't want to cry in front of you."

He moves closer. Puts his hand on my arm. "Do you want me to go?"

"No. It's just—she was so *mean*." I sound like a little

kid. "I-I think she likes pretending I'm not hers. That I'm just her annoying little sister. Granddad's s-second-chance girl."

"Second chance?" Connor moves closer, and gravity and the couch cushions sort of dump us together till we're pressed against each other from hip to knee. "Ivy, the Professor adores you. He brags about you all the time."

I peek out from between my fingers. "He *lies*. Like telling you I'm a writer. I've only written one poem in the last two months. Nothing I've written is good enough to submit, and it only counts if it's good. Milbourns don't do *okay*. It has to be extraordinary."

"Ivy, if I thought everything I wrote had to be *extraordinary*, I would never write anything ever again." Connor shakes his head. "Half of what I write is total shit. You revise it. Or you steal that one good line for another poem. You can't expect yourself to be perfect. It'll just set you up for failure."

I look right at him, at his handsome, square-jawed face and his crooked nose, and I confess my most shameful truth: "That's what I am—a failure."

"What? Why would you say that?" He grabs my hand. "Why would you *think* that?"

"I am. I'm not good at anything." I can't help it; I start crying again. "I love swimming, but I'm not good enough to go to the Olympics. I couldn't even get to state. I love reading, but I'm not a writer, not really. I love baking, but I'm not going to be the next Julia Child. I love languages, but I'm not a natural polyglot. I'm just—mediocre. At *everything*."

Connor is frowning. "You're, what, seventeen? You don't need to have everything figured out. You don't need to have *anything* figured out yet."

Jesus, I hate being patronized. "Dorothea did. Grandmother did. Erica knew what she wanted, even if she was too messed up to make it happen. And you do too." I pull my hand away, annoyed. "You know exactly what you want. And Granddad says you're talented. He doesn't just *say* that, Connor. He doesn't hand out praise lightly. You have to earn it."

"He says it about you," Connor insists. "He's really proud of you. Doesn't he tell you that?"

"No." I can't remember the last time Granddad told me he was proud of me. I was thrilled when I came in second at regionals, but he just said that next year I'd beat that girl from Salisbury. "Whatever I do, I should be doing more or better. I should practice harder, shave a few seconds off my backstroke. I should be journaling every day like Dorothea. I should be writing more poems and submitting them to literary journals. I should be taking classes this summer. Should, should, should. It never ends and I'm so tired of it."

"Have you told him how you feel?" Connor asks.

As if it's that simple. I glare at him. "Is that what you do with your parents? When they ask you what the hell you're going to do with an English degree?"

He has the grace to look ashamed. "No."

"Right." I brush away tears with both hands and stand up. "Can I use your bathroom?"

"Sure." He leads me through a cramped kitchen and down a short hall with two bedrooms and a bathroom. The bathroom is gross, as befits the apartment of two college guys, I guess. I splash cold water on my face and wash my hands, and when I go back out, I feel calmer. I shouldn't have snapped at Connor like that; he was only trying to help.

I peek in the open door of the first bedroom. I suspect it's Connor's because of the two overflowing bookshelves. The bed is unmade, with a green comforter and rumpled blue sheets, and the only other furniture is a beat-up dresser with some framed photos on top.

Connor's footsteps hurry down the hall and I spin around, busted. "Hey. Can I look at your books?"

"Sure." He leads me in and immediately starts making his bed, which I could not care less about. I'm actually more interested in the photos than his books. There's one of him in a graduation robe, flanked by his parents. His dad is tall and broad shouldered and white, with glasses and brown hair and a beard; his mom is tall and curvy and black, and she's wearing a cute turquoise maxi dress.

The picture next to it is of him and a short, skinny old lady with curly gray hair and wrinkled walnut skin. His grams. She beams up at him, the pride shining out of her like rays of sunshine. They clearly adore each another, and my stomach clenches at his loss. The third picture shows his family on the beach: his mom in a blue one-piece swimsuit, his dad in board shorts, Connor, and Ani, who is tall and skinny and could pass for a model in her tiny red bikini.

"Is that your sister? She's gorgeous," I say. *So are you*, I think. In the photo, he's shirtless, his tattoos and abs on full display.

He laughs. "And she knows it. She just turned sixteen and she's such a brat."

"Are you close?" I wonder sometimes what it would be like if I'd grown up with Isobel. We're only two and a half years apart. Would we have fought each other for Granddad's love and attention or bonded over his impossible expectations and been better for it? Would we have been the kind of sisters who borrowed each other's clothes and asked each other for advice about boys?

"Sort of. Ani thinks I'm pretty boring. I was kind of a nerd when I was her age," Connor confesses. "Still am, really."

I scoff and pick up a photo of him and two other tall, muscular boys. "Let me guess—football team?"

Connor laughs. "Yearbook coeditors. I went to a performing arts high school. We didn't have sports teams."

I put the picture back and sit on his freshly made bed. The comforter is really soft. A little thrill runs through me at my bravery. I am in Connor's apartment. Sitting on his bed. I've never been in a boy's bedroom before, unless you count Alex's. But Alex still uses his old brontosaurus sheets sometimes, and his walls are covered with posters of his baseball heroes. This feels so much more grown up.

"Oh. I guess I just assumed... How did you break your nose?"

"I got my ass kicked." Connor shoves his hands in his back pockets. "I was bullied a lot in middle school."

"For what?" I can't imagine him being unpopular.

"Always having my nose stuck in a book. Raising my hand too much in class. Not being black enough—but not being white either. It was bullshit, but I was short and skinny, and I wore glasses, and I talked like an English teacher's kid. I was an easy target."

I lean forward, intrigued. "What changed?"

"I got my nose broken, and Dad took me to the gym and taught me how to box. Next time somebody hit me, I hit him back harder. I got suspended and Grams gave me hell for it, but kids left me alone after that." He shrugs.

"Then I transferred into Duke Ellington for high school. It was okay to be different there. Or maybe there were just more kids like me."

"Middle school sucks. Girls can be pretty vicious too. Not so much with physical fights, but gossip. For me it was all about how my mom was a crazy slut and didn't even know who my dad was."

Connor sinks down next to me on the bed. "You're not your family, Ivy."

"I know." I take a deep breath. "I'm sorry for crying. And for snapping at you. I get so mad when people assume things about me, about my family. I shouldn't have assumed it's always been easy for you. I'm just…jealous. That you're so focused."

He shrugs off the praise. "When I was getting shoved into lockers every day, I decided I was going to become the black J. K. Rowling and those middle school assholes would all be sorry. Then in high school I started writing poetry instead of *Harry Potter* fanfic, so I'm pretty sure I'm not going to end up rich and famous. Oh well."

Now I totally want to read his *Harry Potter* fanfic. "Which Hogwarts house are you?" This is one of my favorite questions. Claire is absolutely Gryffindor; Abby is Hufflepuff.

"Ravenclaw," he says without hesitation. "You?"

"The Sorting Hat *says* Ravenclaw, but I think I'm

probably Hufflepuff." I try to keep the disappointment out of my voice. Hufflepuffs: loyal and kind and hard workers, but not exactly setting the world on fire.

"No way. You're totally Ravenclaw," he insists.

I like the way he sees me. I like that he thinks I'm enough. Just me. Just Ivy.

I lean in, then hesitate because I want to be really clear on this. "Is it okay if I kiss you?"

Connor grins, and for a second I get a glimpse of that shy, nerdy kid he used to be, and I am utterly smitten. "Yeah."

This time we both lean in. His mouth presses against mine, and his arm goes around me, resting on the curve of my hip. I run my hands up over the smooth muscles of his forearms, over his biceps, and he shudders a little beneath my touch. We kiss and kiss, and eventually fall back onto the bed, our legs tangling together.

He kisses his way down my neck, and it tickles, but in a delicious way. When he moves the spaghetti strap of my sundress aside and presses a kiss to my shoulder, it's my turn to shiver. He pauses. "Is this okay?"

"Yes," I say, and he kisses my shoulder again. I trace his side, under his shirt, and he sits up and pulls the shirt off in one swift motion. Shirtless Connor is as hot as I imagined: all lean muscle and the Millay tattoo over his heart. I push him back until he's lying down and I'm leaning over him, tracing the words with my fingertips. Then I stop and read the lines just above his waistband. I explore those too, and the curve of his abdomen, the jut of his hip bones, until he grabs my hand and rolls me over so I'm beneath him.

He braces himself on one forearm, kissing me deeply. I like the weight of him, the feel of us pressed together. It's his turn to skim a hand up over my side, and this time he brushes a hand over my breast and I arch into him. He kisses a trail down my jaw to my ear, to this spot on my neck that feels amazing, down over my bare shoulder. I lean up to give him better access, and he slides my sundress down to my waist so I'm only in my strapless bra. He skims the lines of it, teasing until I'm trembling beneath him. Then he reaches behind me with one hand and unhooks my bra, tossing it aside.

For a nerd, he's sure as hell got game. Even I can't unhook my bra one-handed.

I fall back on the bed and he presses against me, skin to skin, and says my name. I look up at him. I have never been half-naked with anyone before and it's a little scary. But his eyes are admiring. "You're beautiful," he says, and I start to object but he interrupts me with another long, slow kiss. Eventually his mouth moves lower, to my breast, and the things he does with his lips and teeth and tongue have me squirming against him. I can feel him pressing against me through his shorts, and my stomach tightens with want.

And then there are footsteps. "Connor? You home?" a voice calls, followed by the sound of the fridge opening.

"Shit." Connor leaps up. I grab the comforter and pull it over myself. "That's Josh." He raises his voice. "I'll be out in a minute!"

He gets up and yanks on his shirt and then steps out into the hall, pulling the door closed behind him. I scramble to find my bra, which landed on the other side of the bed. I put it back on and wiggle the top of my sundress back up. When I stand and look in the mirror over the dresser, my hair is tangled and my lips are red and my chin is a little sore from Connor's stubble. But I can't stop smiling.

Connor comes back a minute later. "Sorry." He runs a hand over his head, looking embarrassed.

"It's okay." But now that I'm dressed and vertical, I'm thinking again. About going home. About facing my mother and the mess she created. "Are we… What are we? I'm sorry, I should probably play this off like it's no big deal, but—"

Connor leans down and stops my words with a kiss. "Quit apologizing. I want you to be honest with me."

"Sorry, I—" I stop myself and laugh. Claire's always scolding me about that too. "Are you seeing anybody else?"

He shakes his head. "Are you?"

"No. Definitely not. But what about working together?" I take a step back, out of the warm circle of his arms.

Connor's smile fades. "Are you asking me to quit working for the Professor?"

"No, of course not. I know how important that is to you." I would never ask him to choose. "I don't want to quit either. I was just thinking that while we're working, we could keep our relationship more…professional."

If Granddad knew, he would give me speeches designed to keep me from making my mother's mistakes. Lecture me on not letting a boy distract me from writing and swimming and school. Would he feel the need to chaperone us constantly, to know where I am at all times? He certainly wouldn't approve of me being at Connor's apartment. I don't think Connor and I would have gone much further if Josh hadn't come home. I don't think I'm ready. But I'd like to make up my own mind about that.

Connor grabs my hand and pulls me in for another kiss. When we both come up for air, breathing hard, my hands laced around his neck, he grins. "So, just to clarify, none of that?"

I smile up at him. "Definitely more of that. Just not around my family."

"I don't love lying to the Professor. He's been really good to me," Connor says.

"It's not him. My mother… You saw what she's like. If she finds out about us"—I can't help smiling at the word, at the fact that there is an *us*—"she'll make it into something ugly. She poisons everything she touches."

Connor takes my hand in his and I grin up at him, at this new effervescence between us that still feels fragile and as gossamer as a butterfly's wings "Well, if you want to keep it quiet for now, I'm okay with that. We won't let her poison this," he promises.

THIRTEEN

AN HOUR LATER, I WALK THROUGH THE FRONT DOOR WITH A SENSE of dread. Granddad called twice while I was with Connor. I ignored both calls. I never do that, but after that scene Erica made, I think I deserved a few hours to myself without constantly gauging the temperature of the room, without that sick, anxious feeling that spins in my stomach as soon as I see her car in the driveway, without the constant tally in my head of whether the thing I've just said or done is something she would say or do, something a Milbourn girl would say or do.

I'm so tired of the push and pull of living up to Granddad's expectations or down to her example. It doesn't feel like there's any room left for me in between.

"Ivy! Is that you?" Granddad calls, so I reluctantly make my way back to the kitchen. In the living room, a Disney movie murmurs, but Grace has fallen asleep in a nest of pillows, clutching her stuffed puppy. She looks so little. Vulnerable. She deserves a better mother.

So do I.

"Here she is. Liar number three," Isobel mutters with a glare. She and Granddad sit at the kitchen table while Erica leans against the granite counter, her arms folded across her chest. To my surprise, she doesn't have a glass of wine in her hand. Yet.

"Where have you been?" Granddad asks. "Grace said you ran off."

"I went to Abby's." I fiddle with the strap of my sundress and try not to blush as I remember Connor sliding it off my shoulder and tracing its path with his mouth.

I am a terrible liar, but it's not like Granddad is going to guess that I was at Connor's, making out with him and then playing video games with his roommate. Josh is really nice. When he met me, he said, "So *this* is the infamous Ivy," and Connor punched him on the shoulder and told him to shut up. I couldn't stop smiling because that meant Connor was talking about me to his friends, same as I was talking about him to mine.

Granddad frowns. "You didn't answer your phone."

We have a strict rule that when he calls, I pick up. He doesn't check in much, so it's not usually a problem.

"Can you blame me for not wanting to come home after the scene she made?" I ask, waving a hand at Erica.

"I need you to answer the phone when I call you," he says.

"I'm sorry." I drop into the chair between him and Iz. "I just needed some time. I didn't mean to worry you."

"Of course not. You're too responsible for that," Erica mocks.

"Erica, we've already established that this situation is not Ivy's fault."

Great. They've already been fighting about me.

"It is too Ivy's fault. It's all of your faults," Isobel grumbles, and there's some truth to that. We all owe her an apology. "You made such a big deal out of wanting Gracie and me to feel at home here. How are we supposed to do that when you've been lying to us?"

"I understand that we'll need to earn your trust." Granddad folds his hands on the table like he's preparing for an inquisition. "You want to know something, just ask."

Iz only scowls. "That's easy to say *now*. It isn't like you told a little white lie to spare our feelings. This was a huge lie. We have a big sister we never knew about! For fifteen years, I thought *I* was the big sister!" Her voice breaks, her red-rimmed eyes welling up with tears. She swipes at them furiously, and I get the sense she doesn't like crying in front of people any more than I do.

"You are, Iz. You're a great big sister. You always look out for Grace," Erica says, and I am struck by her gentle tone. "The three of us, we're a family. A real family. The kind that sticks together through ups and downs."

Granddad smacks the table with the flat of his hand, and Iz and I both jump in our seats. "That's nonsense and you know it, Erica! I stuck by you through all your mistakes, and we both know there were a hell of a lot. You're the one who walked out, on Ivy and on me."

I fold my hands in my lap so tightly that the knuckles go white. Granddad doesn't lose his temper. He doesn't cuss. He doesn't hit things. This exhibition of temper isn't like him, and I hate that Iz is seeing it without years of kindness to balance it out.

"I didn't have a choice! You were smothering me. I can't breathe in this house. In this town. I was always Dorothea's granddaughter, the Professor's daughter, poor Grace's—" Her voice breaks on her mother's name. "New York, DC—they were perfect. No one knows what a Milbourn is supposed to be. No one gives a damn."

"And that's how you want to live your life? In places where no one cares about you? Don't you find that a little bit sad?" Granddad is a man of strong opinions. He hates comic books and broccoli and people who answer their phones during meals. But I've never heard him like this. Not when I took Alex's "damn fool" dare and jumped from the sunroom roof. Not when one of his favorite students got caught plagiarizing a paper. Not even when he read a biography of Dorothea that included very unflattering things about the history of mental illness in the Milbourn family.

And I see what he's saying, but I also see what Erica's saying about not getting the room you need to grow and change and *be* without the weight of Milbourn history crushing you. I wouldn't put it like she does, but that anonymity…sometimes it looks real appealing.

"I didn't say no one cares about me. I said they don't care that I'm a Milbourn. But I can see how you might have trouble telling the difference." Erica gives him a serpentine smile. "Who would you even be without your wife's name? Without your famous mother-in-law? Some nobody professor in some nothing town."

Granddad takes a deep breath, holding on to his temper by the thinnest leash. "I have never claimed to be a perfect husband or a perfect father." Erica howls with laughter at this, but he plows on. "Or a brilliant scholar, for that matter. Studying Dorothea led me to your mother, and for that I will always be grateful. It gave me three beautiful grandchildren, after all."

"And one fucked-up daughter you'd rather forget," Erica

snaps. "It's not hard to read between those lines. You'll use my girls as your second chance. Your third and fourth chances if I let you. I've got a mind to leave before you sink your claws into them any more than you already have. Did you think I wouldn't find out about the classes you signed my baby up for? Drawing? Gymnastics? Wouldn't want her to get bored, would we? And you're so sorry Iz is missing out on her theater camp. Yeah, right." She turns to Isobel. "Don't believe a word out of his mouth, Iz. It all comes with strings attached. Every goddamn word."

"I don't trust *any* of you. I want to go home." Iz fishes her phone out of her pocket. "I'm calling Dad."

Erica leans over her and plucks the phone from Isobel's hands. "Absolutely not."

Iz gawks at her. "Give it back!"

"Not until you've calmed down." Erica shoves the phone in the back pocket of her jeans. "Rick driving over here tonight is the last thing I need."

"Fine. Whatever." Iz glares. "I'll tell him everything when we see him on Saturday. Then he'll take us home. Gracie and me both."

"Actually," Erica says, "I rescheduled your visit."

Isobel's face falls. "What? *Why?* When did you even talk to him?"

"I called while you were putting the movie on for Grace. Told him we have fun plans with your granddad and it would be disruptive for him to come visit. He was glad to hear you were settling in so well." Erica puts a hand on her daughter's shoulder.

Iz jerks away. "He'll know something's wrong if you don't let us call him. We call him every night before Gracie goes to bed."

"Or he'll think you're busy, having fun with your new friends."

"What new friends?" Iz shouts. "All I do is take care of Gracie while you go off and drink!"

I shrink back. Expect Erica to call her a bitch or slap her or something equally terrible.

Instead Erica shrugs. "Whose fault is that? I didn't ask you to stay in every night. I'm sure Ivy would love to take you to the bonfire this weekend. Wouldn't you, Ivy? Is it Friday or Saturday?"

"I'm not going anywhere with her," Iz snaps.

"Isobel isn't old enough to go to a bonfire party," Granddad says. As if that is the important thing here, asserting family rules.

"Lucky for you, Iz, your grandfather doesn't get to decide that." Erica puts a hand on her daughter's shoulder again. Laying claim. This time Iz sits stiffly beneath her touch. "I don't blame you for not wanting to go with Ivy, honey. I doubt she's any fun at a party. Let's see if we can get the housekeeper's kid to take you."

"His name is Alex, and you leave him out of this," I snap.

"You're awful possessive for a girl who says she's not dating him." Erica's voice is smug as hell. "What do you care if he goes out with your sister?"

"Mama, stop it. I have a boyfriend. I can't go to a party with some other boy!" Iz blushes.

"You think Kyle's going to wait around for you all summer?" Erica laughs. "He's a teenage boy, honey. Save yourself the heartbreak and move on."

"That is terrible advice," I say.

"Like you have so much experience with boys?" Erica asks, and I am so glad—*so glad*—she doesn't know about Connor.

"I hate you. I hate all three of you!" Iz jumps up, pushing her chair back so hard it crashes to the floor, and runs from the room.

I lean over to pick up the chair. "Wow, you're great at this whole mothering thing. I really feel like I missed out."

"Shut up," Erica growls.

Granddad is leaning back and steepling his fingers together. "I'm of a mind to call Rick myself," he says. "It isn't right, Erica, making the girls keep this secret for you. Keeping them away from him. He's Grace's father, and obviously Isobel considers him a father figure too."

"You pick up that phone and I'll never forgive you," Erica snarls. "Whatever you hope is happening here—whatever chance you think you've got to make this right—it'll be gone. Forever."

"Then you've got to do better," Granddad says. "The divorce, moving out here—it's hard on them and you're making it harder."

"So it's all my fault as usual." Erica opens the fridge and takes out a bottle of wine.

"Well, who else's fault would it be?" Granddad asks, throwing up his hands. "No, let me guess. It's my fault. Ivy's. The whole damn town's. Nothing is ever your fault, is it? Sooner or later, you've got to accept responsibility for your choices, Erica. You're the one who keeps saying you're a grown woman. And you're right. You're not a confused, depressed teenager anymore. You've got two children to care for, and you need to start doing a better job of it."

Two children. Even Granddad doesn't count me as hers.

I'm sitting right between them, but I feel invisible. They could argue about me and Gracie and Iz all day long, but my feelings—what I have to say—wouldn't really matter.

Granddad watches as Erica opens the wine and pours a very full glass. "I know you've always been resistant to therapy, but maybe it's time to think about professional help. Rehab. If you don't want the girls to go to Rick, they could stay here with me."

"You'd love that, wouldn't you?" Erica takes a very long sip of wine, then nods at me. "I already gave you one kid. Wasn't she enough?"

I wasn't. I never am. No matter what I do or how hard I try.

If Granddad had custody of Gracie and Iz, even temporarily, I bet he'd be able mold *them* into perfect Milbourn girls. An actress. An artist—or maybe a gymnast. But at what cost?

The thing is, part of me wants him to turn the weight of his expectations on them and leave me be. When did my thinking get so twisted? When did I become a person who's willing to sacrifice my little sisters to get some peace?

Granddad and Erica are still arguing. I head for the sanctuary of my room, and neither of them says a word. I wonder how long it will take for them to notice my absence.

The living room is dark, the movie is off, and Gracie is gone. Upstairs, I pause in the hall outside my sisters' bedroom. Raise my fist and knock quietly on their door. "It's Ivy," I say.

I know they're in there—can hear someone's footsteps— but no one answers or comes to open the door.

Why didn't I tell them the truth that first day? Regret fills my throat. I'm a terrible sister.

I pace the stuffy attic like a restless cat, too frustrated to even cry. I pick up the prom picture of Alex and me on my nightstand. If we were talking, I could run down to the carriage house. Luisa would make me dinner and Alex would make me laugh and I'd feel better. But no. He's still sulking because I want to kiss another boy. As though all I ever was to him was a potential girlfriend.

I shove the picture in the drawer. I don't want to see his stupid face right now.

I sit at my desk and pull out last year's Christmas journal. Yesterday, after Granddad interrupted our lunch, I scribbled a poem about Connor. About wanting him. My own words make me blush. Maybe there's a little bit of Dorothea in me after all.

I open my laptop, drumming my fingers impatiently while a bookmarked page loads. I compose a new email, following the submission guidelines. The deadline is midnight. Publication is online only, not print—but it's a start. I hit Send.

CHAPTER
FOURTEEN

The secret is out, but the house still feels like it's holding its breath.

I find myself sneaking around on tiptoe, wary of every creak and groan of the old floorboards. The sense of doom that descended the night of the storm, the night I found out Erica was coming back, still hasn't lifted.

I skip my swim the next morning and stay in my room, refreshing my email constantly to see if I've heard back from the literary magazine yet (even though I know it will probably be a while). I'm not sure whether I'm more afraid of being accepted or rejected. In the afternoon, I force myself to go out to the dock. I swim for a bit and then spread my towel out on the sun-bleached wooden boards.

Remind myself that I am a salt-and-sunshine girl, and this hurricane gloom won't last. Erica brought it with her, and when she leaves—and she will, I know it—she'll take it with her.

Part of me hopes Alex will stroll up with that cocky grin of his and challenge me to a race across the channel. I stare at the windows of the carriage house, the blinds pulled shut to block out the heat, willing him to appear. His beat-up black pickup is in the driveway, so I know he's probably home, but there's no sign of him.

Maybe he's hanging out with the guys from the baseball team. I saw Ty pick him up late last night. I wonder what Alex told them about us. About me. Would he say I led him on? That I was a tease, letting him hold my hand, then telling him I wanted to be with somebody else? Some college boy? I don't want to think that he'd bad-mouth me to save face. Still, he bragged about hooking up with Ginny. And he was so angry when he saw me with Connor.

I'm not sure what I'm more worried about: the whole town thinking I'm a slut like my mother or *Alex* thinking that. *For somebody who's worked so hard to be nothing like your mom, you're sure acting a lot like her.* Much as I tell myself that he was just mad and lashing out, those words have stuck with me.

When I hear Erica's car rumble down the driveway, I go back inside. Grab Grace from the couch in the sunroom where she's been reading one of my old Fancy Nancy books. We make chocolate-chip cookies and sandwich vanilla ice cream between them, and she says she's sad not to see her daddy this weekend but she's glad we're sisters.

She's much easier to win over than Isobel, who's wallowing in their room, not tempted by the scents of chocolate and sugar and butter wafting up the stairs, or the fact that Luisa went out and got fat-free frozen yogurt just for her.

"She said she doesn't want to pretend we're a happy family," Gracie reports back, her little shoulders drooping beneath her pink T-shirt. "But I'm not pretending. I like it here."

"I'm glad, 'cause I like having you here," I say, tweaking one of her braids. Much as I hate every moment Erica is here, I am grateful for the chance to get to know my little sister. She's sweet and easygoing and cheerful. But sometimes I wonder how much of that sweetness is her feeling like she has to make up for all the anger around her.

"I wish I could do something to cheer Izzy up," Grace says. "Maybe I'll draw her a picture."

"I bet she'd like that." I wrap the extra ice cream cookie-wiches in parchment paper and put them in the freezer. It's strange to have extras instead of running down to the carriage house and giving them to Alex. If he were around, he'd eat at least two. "But it's not your job to make sure everybody is okay. You're a little girl. It's the grown-ups' job to make sure *you're* okay."

The irony is not lost on me. How many times have *I* been the one frantically trying to please? I'm just a little more subtle about it at seventeen than she is at six.

Gracie smiles. "That's what Izzy says too. Sometimes people are in bad moods and there's nothing you can do about it."

After ice cream sandwiches, Gracie goes back to her book and I do the dishes, wondering what her life was like in DC. Were there slammed doors and fights and ominous silences there too? Was Erica the one to initiate the separation, or was her husband? Frankly, I can't imagine anyone putting up with her for seven years, but maybe she hasn't always been like this. Isn't that what she keeps saying? That it's our fault, not hers? I don't want to believe it, but—

"Hey there, chickadee," Luisa says, coming in with a load of laundry.

"You should get a raise," I point out. "You're taking care of five of us now."

"Don't you worry. The Professor already offered me one." She nods at the dishes. "You can leave those if you want. I'll get them."

"It's good thinking time," I say. There's no reason I can't do my own dishes.

"What's on your mind?" She sets the basket down on

the kitchen table and begins to fold towels: Granddad's brown ones, the pink polka-dot ones that showed up with Grace, the blue ones I now share with Erica and Iz.

"How's Alex?" I ask, instead of answering. Though maybe that's an answer in itself.

"Been in a mood all week. Going out with his friends from the baseball team a lot after work." I try to hide my frown. Alex works part-time at the hardware store's garden center. That leaves a lot of time for hanging out with the guys, drinking beer, and potentially trash-talking me. "I noticed he hasn't been around here much. Did something happen at the party last weekend? You two get in a fight?"

I rinse the metal measuring spoons, considering how to answer. I want to talk to her, but I don't want to put her in the middle. "You should probably ask him."

"I did, but he's a teenage boy. He won't tell me anything. And he's not the only one I worry about." Luisa's voice is soft. Kind. So different from my mother's. "Heard there's another party tonight. You going?"

I busy myself scrubbing the cookie sheet. "I am. I sort of...have a date."

Connor put his number in my phone yesterday, and we've been texting all day, sending each other silly pictures: him making coffee at Java Jim's, my chocolate-chip ice cream sandwiches, a selfie of me and Grace. He and I are going to the bonfire together. I didn't want him to pick me up, so we're meeting there. At what he referred to as "our" bench.

"I thought it might be something like that," Luisa says, and I spin around, half expecting to see accusation in her eyes, but I don't. She's sporting a big smile. "Someone special?"

"Maybe. I—you know I love Alex, but—"

"But not like that," she finishes. "That's okay, honey. You don't have to apologize for your feelings. You can't make yourself fall in love with somebody."

She's being so nice that I want to cry. Tears actually start gathering in my eyes and I brush them away with the back of my hand, embarrassed. "Don't tell Granddad, okay?"

She stops folding. "About your date? Is it someone he wouldn't approve of?"

"It's Connor." I know she's heard Granddad talk about Connor, even if she hasn't met him yet. I think she'd like him. But I'm kind of biased.

"His student? The one you're working on that project with?" Luisa laughs. "I know the Professor can be strict about boys, but I don't think he'd have a problem with that. Why don't you want to tell him?"

"I don't know." I brush my hair behind my ears with wet, soapy fingers. "It's still so new. I don't want him weighing in on it yet."

"Well, if Connor is important to you, it won't stay secret

for long. You can't keep the different parts of your life in little boxes, all nice and neat," Luisa says. "Especially with him working for your granddad. But I see what you're saying. There's a lot going on around here. Connor makes you happy?"

I smile, remembering how he sent me a picture of a poem he was reading. I don't know any other boy who would do that. "Yeah. He does."

.....

The walk through town feels...fraught. As if everyone is watching and whispering. I try to convince myself that I'm being silly, that no one cares about the scene Erica made in the coffee shop yesterday. Still, when I see Mrs. Summers heading my way with a picnic basket and her bulldog, Quincey, trotting along beside her, I have to fight the urge to duck down an alley.

"Ivy, sweetheart," she says. Quincey sits, panting, his pink tongue lolling out. "How are you doing?"

"I'm okay. How are you? On your way to the concert in the square? Judy says that bluegrass band is real good."

"I'm fine, sweetheart. I just want you to know"—she puts a sympathetic hand on my forearm—"that scene your mama made yesterday was appalling. Really. The way she spoke to you and your sisters! Mr. Summers had to practically hold me down to keep me from going over there and giving her a piece of my mind."

"Thank you." I can't imagine what Erica would have done. Probably cussed the old lady out for interfering. "I doubt she would've listened to you though."

"Well, I'd still like to give her what-for. Imagine a mother talking to her children like that! Calling you a *b-i-t-c-h*!" I stifle a smile. Once a third-grade teacher, always a third-grade teacher, I guess. "But then we all know she isn't much of a mother, is she? Leaving you like she did. How long are they in town for? Is Erica back for good?"

Oh, now we get to the heart of the matter. My smile fades. "No. Just the summer. If they stay that long." Whenever Erica leaves the house, part of me thinks she might not come back. That she'll drive off and disappear and leave the girls behind. Would it be so bad if she did? I survived it, but I was so little. It would be harder for Gracie and Iz.

"I had Erica in class, same as you, you know. She was mean even then. Bullied the other girls." Mrs. Summers beams at me. "Nothing like you. You were always so bright. And sweet as pie."

That's me. Sweet as pie. "Thank you, Mrs. Summers." I edge away, almost tripping over Quincey's leash. "Excuse me. I'm meeting someone. I don't want to be late."

"Oh, is it that nice black boy who works at the coffee

shop? Jules said she saw the two of you walking past the bank yesterday holding hands. What's his name? Colin?"

Jesus. If I had any doubts about how fast gossip spreads in this town, they are extinguished.

"Connor," I correct. Jules is Mrs. Summers's daughter who works over at the SunTrust. She is at least forty years old, and you'd think she would have better things to do at work than notice who I walk down the street holding hands with.

"He seems real nice," Mrs. Summers says. "And things are different than they were when I was young."

Meaning what? That Connor and I can date, even though he's biracial and I'm white? That it's not the fifties, so I won't be disowned and he won't be run out of town—or worse? "Thanks. Well, I don't want to keep you. Bye!"

I scurry away. This is the part of Cecil I'd be happy to escape. The small-mindedness. The gossip. I was stupid to think I could keep our relationship secret. Nothing stays secret in this town for long. Didn't I tell my mother that?

By the time I meet Connor at our bench, it's almost dusk.

He's scribbling in his Moleskine again, but he shoves it in his back pocket and scrambles to his feet when he sees me.

"Hi." I smile up at him bashfully, then go up on my tiptoes for a kiss. Which turns into a couple kisses. "I've been waiting to do that all day."

"Me too. Nice dress." His eyes scan me appreciatively from head to toe, and I spin around to show the dress off. Claire helped me pick it out for the sports awards banquet, so it's a little sexier than anything I would have chosen on my own. The front is a modest halter, but the back dips down low, then swirls out and ends right above my knees.

"Thank you. You look pretty nice yourself." He's wearing jeans and a button-down red shirt, sleeves rolled up to the elbows, that sets off his brown skin. I lace my arms around his neck. He smells piney, like maybe he went home after work and shaved and did whatever boys do before a first date. "You also smell nice."

Connor buries his nose in my hair. "You always smell like summer. It drove me crazy when we were working together at your house that day we made lunch. Your hair smells like coconut."

He presses a kiss to the hollow of my neck, and a shiver runs up my spine.

He gestures at the cove. "You want to go over to the party?"

"I guess. I mean, yes. Claire is dying to meet you." Abby's at the Crab Claw till close; I might not get to see her because of my curfew. I look down the marina, to the restaurants that jut out over the water. Their decks are full of tourists and boaters and couples out for a nice dinner, all enjoying the pretty weather. There's no chance of her getting off early. "But I like being alone with you."

And I don't want to run into Charlotte Wu or Katie Griffith or anyone else who witnessed the scene with my mother—or has heard about it second or thirdhand.

"Me too." Connor's voice is low. "We could leave early and go back to my place for a while. If you want. No pressure."

"I want," I remind him, pulling his head down for another kiss. His arms go around me, his fingers tracing little circles on my lower back, and we don't break apart until some guys walk past and holler at us to get a room.

"Jesus. Are we that couple?" I bury my face in my hands, embarrassed.

"The ones who can't keep their hands off each other? I'm kind of okay with that." He grins.

"I've never been that couple before. Not that I have a lot of experience being a couple." I went out with Jake Usilton in ninth grade for a couple weeks. We went to the movies once and he held my hand and bought me a Coke. Then he decided he liked Riley West better. That's pretty much all of my dating experience. "Do you? I mean, have you had many girlfriends?"

Presumably he learned how to kiss like that from someone.

"I had one girlfriend in high school, my junior and senior years. Ruby. We were pretty serious," Connor says, and I wonder if "pretty serious" means they had sex. Probably. I mean, two years is a long time to date.

"We broke up last fall. She was up at NYU and the long-distance thing didn't work. I applied to some schools in New York too, but I got a better scholarship to come here. Couldn't pass that up, especially with my parents looking at..." He frowns.

"Looking at what?" I ask.

He runs a hand over his closely shaven hair. "Grams has her own apartment in our basement, but if she keeps getting worse, my mom's not going to be able to take care of her, even with a part-time nurse to help out. They'll have to hire somebody full time. Or put her in an Alzheimer's unit. Stuff like that's not cheap."

"I'm sorry." I bite my lip, feeling guilty that I don't have to worry about money. And feeling jealous of Ruby, who was talented enough to get into a performing arts high school and then brave enough to go to NYU.

"Anyway," Connor continues, "I can write anywhere. And it worked out great because your grandfather is a pretty amazing mentor. I'd never get this kind of opportunity at a bigger school."

"I submitted a poem yesterday," I blurt out like a completely self-absorbed idiot. "Of mine. To an online lit mag."

"Really? That's great. Which one?" he asks, and we start toward the party, hand in hand, while I tell him about it.

To our right, the sun sets into the Bay in a riot of

cotton-candy blues and pinks, and the air is soft and balmy and tinged with salt and fish. I don't know why I'm not happier.

"You were so adamant about poetry not being your thing," he teases me.

"I was inspired," I say, which I guess is true—he inspires me—but I pull him to a stop just short of the rocks that separate the cove from the marina. I could keep walking, keep pretending that he and Granddad know me better than I know myself. But that's not what I want from this. "That's not true. I freaked out because Erica and Granddad were fighting and she said some really mean things. I was proving a point by submitting that poem. Or trying to, anyhow."

"Ivy." Connor leans in and cups my face in his hands. "You don't have anything to prove with me. I'm not with you because you're a Milbourn, okay?"

"Okay," I say in a small voice. "But why are you? With me, I mean?"

I'm ruining this before it even gets started. I'm being too needy. *You're the kind of people who drive everyone away.*

But Connor grins that big, boyish grin that lights up his whole face. "Because you're smart and beautiful and generous, and you love poetry, and you put up with a lot of shit from the people around you without losing yourself, and you don't call me out for being pretentious, and you're incredibly forthright but also shy, and you're a really good listener." He rattles it all off in a rush and then looks down at the sandy path.

"Oh." I don't know what to say. "Thank you."

"Anytime." He helps me over the rocks into the cove. "So, Claire. Is she the one who's afraid of birds?"

I laugh. "Yeah. But she's also pretty fierce, so don't let her scare you off, okay?"

He threads his fingers through mine. "I don't scare easily."

Claire sees us and comes running despite her strappy four-inch heels. She's wearing this gorgeous emerald-green jumper with a plunging neckline, and I don't know how she manages to pull it off but somehow she does.

"Hi. You must be Connor. I'm Claire. It's so nice to meet you." She gives him a predator's smile. "If you hurt my friend, I'll murder you in your sleep."

"Claire!" I groan.

"Noted," Connor says, letting go of my hand to shake hers. "It's nice to meet you. I appreciate loyalty."

"Good. Would you fetch us some cheap wine, please, so we can talk about you?" Claire pulls some cash out of her wristlet to chip in for the collection.

He laughs, waving off her money. "I've got it." He brushes a kiss on my cheek and strolls off toward the keg and the coolers.

"Chivalrous. I like it," Claire says. "And you're right. He's hot. Do I need to give you the sex talk?"

I groan again. "Jesus. No. You gave me the sex talk when we were eleven."

She smiles, remembering. "You were horrified."

"I was *eleven*. And before you ask, yes, I am still on the pill." Claire preached about the wonders of it regulating my cycle and helping with cramps until I asked Luisa to take me to her gynecologist.

"Use a condom too. Just in case. You can't be too careful. Do you know his sexual history? Has he been tested?" she asks.

I blush. "Claire. This is our first date. We're not having sex yet."

"Yet! You said *yet*," she crows, and I glance around, making sure that no one is close enough to overhear us. I knew these questions would be forthcoming because Claire is Claire, but I didn't think she'd bring it up *right now*. I shrug, caught between mortification and wanting to talk about it with her. Truth is, I've never thought about having sex with someone before. I've wondered what sex would be like, but the other person was always kind of...amorphous.

If this lasts (please let it last), I could see Connor being my first. I could see him bringing the same passion and attention and sweetness to sex as he does to everything else. Which is pretty hot. I've had a lot of fantasies about it in the last twenty-four hours, honestly.

Fantasies that I imagine will remain just that for a while. Fantasies that I don't want to discuss in the middle of a crowded party.

"Remember, if you're not ready to talk about it, you're not ready to do it!" Claire sings out.

"I know, I know. And I'm not ready, so can we please change the subject?" I beg.

"Okay. Do you think Cooper Sutton's cute?" She nods to a blond guy wearing a white polo, Nantucket Reds, and boat shoes.

"I don't know. He's not really my type," I say.

She tilts her head, considering. "He and Jenna broke up last weekend."

Jenna and Coop were the prom prince and princess. They are relentlessly popular and—like Abby and Ty—have dated since the seventh grade. If Claire even looks sideways at Coop, I guarantee Jenna will throw a fit. Unfortunately, Coop is totally Claire's type: rich and pretty and kind of a douche bag.

"Speaking of…" I nod as Jenna makes a beeline for us.

"Ivy! Hey!" Jenna squeals as though we are friends. "Who's the guy who came with you?"

"Connor?" He would explain my sudden rise in social status.

"Her boyfriend," Claire adds helpfully.

"Oh." Jenna's face falls. "I was hoping he was like

your cousin or something. He's really hot, and I'm single now, so—"

"Sorry, he's taken," Claire says with not an ounce of sorry in her voice.

"Got it. No worries. I don't poach." Jenna smiles at me, and I can see Claire bristling at the notion that Connor could be "poached," but Jenna sails on. "Where'd you find him? Does he go to the college?" I nod and she purses her glossy red lips. "Cool. If he has any hot friends, let me know."

"Sure." I nod again. Tonight is going to be full of bizarre conversations, I guess.

Jenna starts to walk away, then hesitates. "Bummer about your mom being back in town. I heard she's a total bitch." She walks away without waiting for me to respond.

"I have known Connor for all of five seconds, and I can tell he would never in a million years go for someone like Jenna," Claire says.

I smile. "I'm not worried. But hey, I thought we weren't supposed to judge other girls."

"Busted." Claire laughs, then nods in the direction of the keg. "Hey, did Alex bring a date?"

I turn my head and gawk. "That isn't his date. That's my sister."

"That's Isobel?"

Iz is wearing jeans and a black tank top with a couple of

long necklaces. She looks boho cute with her hair in two braids. I wonder if Erica asked Alex to bring her. And I wonder why he said yes. To be polite? To make me jealous because he's hanging out with my sister and not me?

It works. I watch as he introduces her to half the baseball team and their girlfriends. Katie Griffith says something that makes Iz laugh, while I remember the look of horror on Katie's face at the coffee shop. Was Katie the one who told Jenna that my mom's a bitch? Does everybody in our class know by now? Do they all feel sorry for me?

Alex looks up as if he can feel my eyes on him, and I think he might smile. Wave. Nod his head in acknowledgment. *Something.* Instead, he looks away.

"You two still aren't talking?" Claire asks, but the answer is pretty evident. "I can't believe he's ghosting on you like this. You don't think he'd hook up with Isobel to get back at you, do you?"

"No. He's not like that." I'm questioning lots of things about my friendship with Alex, but not that.

Connor returns, carrying two cups of wine and a beer tucked into the crook of his arm. He hands one cup to Claire and one to me and then slides his arm around me.

I slip away from him. "My sister's here. With Alex."

"Oh." He frowns. "Is this not a date anymore?" I follow his gaze to Iz and Alex. Iz is laughing and holding a beer. She looks pretty, unfettered by the tension of home.

"I'm afraid she'll say something to Erica." But I note the tightness in Connor's jaw, the way he's shifted away from me. "This isn't about Alex. Alex knows—well, I don't know if he knows we're dating, because he's not speaking to me. But I don't care if he finds out. He knows I'm not interested in dating *him*."

"You sure about that? He seemed pretty possessive when he interrupted lunch."

"Oh, he knows," Claire says. "Ivy made it clear last weekend when she told him it was none of his business who she kisses. It made my feminist heart go pitter-pat—especially coming from Ivy."

"What's that supposed to mean, *especially coming from Ivy*?" I ask.

"That you don't like telling people the truth when it will disappoint them." Claire gives me a grin that shows off her dimples. "That you're not a bitch like me. Hey, could you just ask Isobel not to tell your mom?"

"I don't think we're sharing sisterly secrets yet." Honestly, I don't know if we'll ever get there. Will the girls stay around long enough for us to start feeling like a real family? Or will Erica get fed up with Granddad's rules and take off? I'm practically holding my breath, waiting for the fight that takes them out of our lives again, maybe forever.

I don't know how I'd feel about that anymore. I'd be glad to see Erica go, but Iz? Gracie?

"I don't like keeping you a secret," Connor says.

"This isn't some possessive alpha-male thing, is it?" Claire asks, sipping her wine.

"No, this is an 'I'm crazy about this girl and would like to hold her hand in public' thing," Connor says, and I think even Claire's icy heart melts.

I hold out my hand. What the hell. If Jenna Martin and Mrs. Summers know Connor and I are dating, it won't be long before all of Cecil knows—including Erica and Granddad.

Connor looks at me, his eyes hopeful. "Are you sure?"

I lean over and kiss him, and his grin afterward is its own reward.

But I dart another worried glance in Iz's direction. "I can't believe Erica let her come... No, I totally believe it. But it seems like a bad idea, right? She's only fifteen, and she's mad at the world. Anger and beer and our family's history do not go well together."

"Do you want to talk to her?" Connor asks.

I shake my head. "She wouldn't listen."

"Well, I'll keep an eye on her. While I'm keeping an eye on Coop," Claire says, with a fiendish smile. "You two have fun, okay?"

"Claire. Do not hook up with Coop, or Jenna will murder *you* in your sleep!"

Claire laughs. "No promises!"

"Josh is over there with Jay and Nia. You want to go say hi?" Connor asks.

"Sure. I'd love to meet more of your friends," I say, gripping his hand a little tighter, hoping they'll be nice. Hoping they'll like me and not think it's dumb that he's dating some high school girl. Hoping Granddad hasn't failed any of them. Connor guides us to a corner of the cove, where his roommate is sitting on a blanket with another guy and a girl.

"Connor! Ivy! Hey," Josh says, scooting over to make room for us. He's tall and skinny with floppy, dark hair and glasses and a Superman T-shirt—the kind of adorable I expected Connor would be before we met.

"Ivy, this is Jayden, this is Nia, and you've already met Josh," Connor says.

"Girl, that is an amazing dress," Jayden says. "Twirl for me!"

I oblige and he whistles and Nia elbows him. She's tall and pretty, with a gorgeous Afro. "Ignore Jay. He's had one too many peach chardonnays."

"You're drinking peach chardonnay? Seriously?" Josh shakes his head.

"Like your hipster IPAs are better?" Jay frowns as we sit down. "Oh shit, I bet Ivy's going to be good at this game. I had your grandfather's Southern Women Writers class last semester and he was hard-core. The man gave me a B!"

"He gives everybody Bs. Except for Connor," I point

out, and they all laugh and then Josh explains the rules. They're playing some kind of drinking game that involves a deck of cards with picture prompts on them. The goal is to tell a story based on the picture cards in your hand. Every time you falter, you have to draw another card and drink. I'm nervous that my story will be stupid, but then Josh starts telling a tale of a wizard trapped in a castle with a poisoned apple, which makes absolutely no sense after only three cards, and my competitive urge kicks in. This is going to be fun.

·····

I don't win the first game (that would be Connor), but I don't lose either (that would be Josh). My worries about being too awkward or too, I don't know, *high school* are unfounded. Everyone in the group is totally nice and welcoming. Apparently, last year they all lived in the creative arts dorm as freshmen. Nia's a dance major. Josh and Jay are both potential English majors.

Jay is telling a story about two hot African princes that is only loosely inspired by his card and lamenting how finding another cute gay black man in this town is like finding a needle in a haystack. Connor is holding my hand, tracing circles on my palm. The air smells like roasting hot dogs and burnt marshmallows, and the breeze blowing in off the Bay sends clouds scudding over the half-moon. Taylor Swift plays on someone's speakers, and a few feet away, the waves sing a lullaby to the pebbly shore. I think I could stay like this all night. Maybe forever.

Then someone taps my shoulder.

I look up, startled. Alex is towering over me. "We need to talk."

CHAPTER
FIFTEEN

NOW? ALEX WANTS TO TALK *NOW?*

"It's about your sister," he clarifies, and I search the shadows behind him for Iz. She's huddled a few yards away with Claire. Leaning against Claire half-mast, like her head is too heavy to hold up.

I jump to my feet. "Did you get Isobel *drunk?*"

"I am not responsible." Alex holds his hands out. "She poured her own drinks. She said she was okay!"

"She's *fifteen!*" I turn to Connor and his friends. "It was really nice to meet you all. I'm sorry. I have to go take care of my sister."

"We've all been there. Water and Advil. And carbs. Lots of carbs," Nia advises.

Connor stands. "Let me come with you. I'll walk you two home."

"I've got this." Alex is white-knuckling his beer.

"Clearly you don't or my little sister wouldn't be trashed." I stalk over to Claire and Isobel. "What happened?"

"I don't feel good," Iz whines.

I check my phone. We've got forty-five minutes till curfew. "How much did you have to drink?"

"Three beers. Four?" She looks to Alex.

"I didn't know I had to keep track," he says tightly.

"I'm sorry, Ivy. I got a little distracted gossiping about Jenna and Coop," Claire apologizes.

"It's okay." Iz is my sister, not hers. It was my job to keep an eye on her.

If Granddad is waiting up for us, he is going to be *pissed*.

"Would you get her a hot dog, please?" I ask Connor, and he heads for the bonfire.

"What can I do?" Alex asks. "Let me do something."

"You've done enough. We've got it from here."

"'We,' huh? Thought you weren't dating him."

I count to ten. "Yes, we're dating. I like Connor, and I'm dating him, and you're going to have to deal with it, okay?"

"Or what? We can't be friends anymore if I don't like the guy?" Alex asks.

"I thought you didn't want to be friends anymore." I whirl on him. "Go away, Alex."

He looks at me for a long minute, and then he leaves.

"Hot dogs are like a million calories," Iz is protesting. "Where's Alex going? He's nice. Mama made him bring me, but he was nice about it."

"What have you had to eat today?" I ask. "Please tell me it was more than a grapefruit and some lettuce."

"None of your damn business." She tries to get in my face and almost falls over. Claire steadies her. "I like you. You're nice. Nicer than her."

Claire cackles. "Oh, that is so not true. Ivy's the nicest."

"Nuh-uh. She's a liar." Iz hiccups. "Everybody's a fucking liar. Kyle. Granddad. Ivy. Mama... Mama's the worst. Only sometimes, the terrible things she says are true."

"How do you mean?" Claire asks. Iz hiccups again, and Claire rubs her back.

"She said Kyle wasn't going to wait for me all summer, and I think she's right. I've only been gone a week and Rhiannon says he was already flirting with Emma Sinclair," Iz says. "Maybe if I were skinnier, he wouldn't break up with me. Mama says I should lay off the chocolate-chip cookies. Or maybe if I gave him a blow job."

"Oh fuck no." Claire hauls my sister around by the elbow and stares at her. "You are so pretty. Your mama doesn't know what she's talking about. Some people are just big black holes of need, and they'll suck all the happiness right out of you if you let them. My father's like that. I mean, do you see your mama in a happy relationship? No, you do not. You are gorgeous, baby girl. Don't you ever let her tell you any different."

"Can I tell you a secret?" Isobel is drunk-whispering, which means I can hear her perfectly from several feet away.

"Of course. I'm a good secret keeper," Claire says.

"Sometimes I hate her." Isobel's lip quivers. "She was like this when she and my bio dad broke up. She got drunk all the time and she lost her job and she got *mean*. I had to do everything—make dinner, do laundry, walk to school. All by myself. I was *seven*." She looks at me. "Sometimes I think you're lucky 'cause you got to grow up without her. Is that terrible?"

"No." Claire and I say it together.

"What changed?" I ask.

"My teacher threatened to call Child Protective Services," Iz slurs. "But she didn't quit drinking till she met Dad."

Connor comes back with a bottle of water and a blackened hot dog on a roasted bun.

"Thank you," I say, handing the hot dog to Iz. "Here. Eat."

She wrinkles her nose. "I'm not eating bread."

"Eat the damn bread, Isobel. I can't take you home like this. Granddad will pitch a fit."

She glares at me. "Mama won't care. She drinks all the time."

"There's so much wrong with that…I don't even know where to start," I mutter.

"What did I say about eating whatever you want?" Claire asks.

Iz glowers at her too. "Like *you* eat hot dogs. Look at you!"

"Are you kidding? I love hot dogs." Claire grabs the hot dog from Iz and takes an enormous bite. Mustard drips onto her green jumper but she just shrugs. "See? Your turn. Come on, Iz. It'll make you feel better."

Iz takes the hot dog and nibbles at it. Connor is standing close, his shoulder brushing mine, lending silent support.

"And that better be the only wiener you put in your mouth. We do *not* give blow jobs so that boys will like us!" Claire roars, and Connor nearly chokes on his beer.

Iz stares at Claire like she's found a new hero. "Okay."

· · · · ·

"You want me to come in with you?" Claire whispers forty-five minutes later.

We're standing outside my front door. The TV murmurs through the open living room windows, but the lamp is on in the library, so my chances are fifty-fifty of running into Granddad at either entrance. I'm hoping I can sneak Isobel in the front door and up the stairs before he sees her. "No, I've got it. But thank you."

"I'll come by tomorrow and check on you," she says to Iz, stroking her messy blond curls. Iz nestles into her, and I think what a good big sister Claire would be (unlike me). "Feel better, okay?"

Iz mumbles an incoherent response. Claire practically dragged her home. I tried to help but Iz wouldn't let me touch her. And she threw up in somebody's garden.

"Night, Ivy Bear," Claire says, and I give her a hug. I am damn lucky to have a friend like her.

Still, this is not how I'd hoped my night would end.

"All right. Time to go inside," I say to Iz as Claire disappears down the dark driveway. "You go straight up to the bathroom and brush your teeth. I'll be up in a minute with water and ibuprofen." I get out my keys, but the front door is unlocked, which means Granddad is still up. Super.

"I'm sleepy," Iz complains, her eyes drifting closed as she leans against the white bricks.

"I know." I swing open the door quietly. "Go upstairs now. Quiet, okay?"

Ignoring me, Iz creeps to the living room and peers in the doorway. "Iz. Go upstairs!" I hiss, looking to see what's caught her attention.

Erica's fallen asleep on the couch. The TV sends flickering ghosts over her face. In sleep, she looks young. Softer. Her face loses some of its armor; her lipstick has worn off and left her mouth vulnerable. The wine bottle she opened before supper is sitting empty on the coffee table, a glass next to it. The front windows are open, letting in the cool night breeze. Someone—Granddad?—has tucked Great-Grandmother's quilt over her, and she's snuggled into it.

When I'm sick, Granddad brings me ginger ale, tucks that quilt around my shoulders, and watches BBC adaptations of Jane Austen with me. He probably did the same thing—or some variation of it—for my mother when she was young. For the first time, it hits me, viscerally: he's her father. He might not always like her, but he still loves her. Despite all the heartbreaks, he's willing to give her another chance.

"Girls?"

I spin around. Granddad has snuck up behind us in his stockinged feet.

Iz wobbles and almost falls. I catch her elbow, but she yanks away.

Granddad narrows his eyes. "Isobel, have you been drinking?"

She raises her chin. "Yep."

At least she's smart enough not to deny it.

He herds us down the hall. The framed pictures of Dorothea getting married, getting her PhD, and getting her Pulitzer Prize watch our shameful progression. "I knew it was a bad idea for you to go out tonight. Ivy, what were you thinking, letting her drink like that?"

Of course. Of course this is my fault. Did I pour the beer down her throat?

"I didn't see her until it was too late," I mutter.

Granddad shakes his head while I get Iz a glass of water. "The cove isn't that big, Ivy. Last week you came home smelling like liquor and now... Isobel, I know your mother hasn't set a good example for how to drink responsibly, but you're too young to—Isobel, are you listening to me?" Granddad waves a hand in front of her face to catch her attention, and Iz's droopy eyes snap open. "You're grounded."

She shrugs. "So? I have no life here anyway. Mama still has my phone."

"That's part of the problem. You need a life outside your phone. Theater camp starts on Monday morning, and you're going," Granddad decides. "You need to meet people your own age and be productive."

Productive. Like the secret to happiness is crossing things off a to-do list.

"I don't want to be in their stupid *Peter Pan*," she whines.

"Then you can help paint sets or sew costumes or whatever else they need," Granddad says. "You'll be at camp every Monday through Friday for the next four weeks, 10:00 a.m. until 2:00 p.m. And when you get home, you'll have a list of chores to do before dinner."

Iz wrinkles her nose. "Chores! Why? You have a housekeeper!"

"This will be a wonderful chance for you to get to know Luisa," Granddad says.

Poor Luisa, saddled with Iz, I think. But then I feel ashamed. Luisa has been like a mom to me: loving, encouraging, stern when I needed it. We laugh a lot together. She listens to me. Doesn't Iz deserve someone like that too?

"I'm sure she'll appreciate the help now that there are twice as many people for her to look after," Granddad continues. "There are rules in this house, Isobel, and there are consequences for breaking them. As long as you're under this roof, I will not have you coming home drunk. It's reckless and dangerous and—"

Isobel glares at him. "Mama doesn't care. She didn't even wait up for me."

"Well, *I* care. Erica and I are going to have a long talk tomorrow about the kind of example she's setting," Granddad says grimly.

Isobel slumps against the wall. "What about Ivy? She was drinking too."

"Ivy and I are going to have our own talk. You get to bed." Granddad takes her water glass and refills it. "We'll discuss this again tomorrow, in the event that your memory is hazy."

Isobel glowers at us before stumbling out of the kitchen.

Granddad waits until we hear her feet on the stairs before turning to me. "I had one cup of wine," I say. "*One*. I heard you last week, loud and clear. You can ask me to recite the alphabet backward if you want."

"I believe you, but what about your sister? What were you doing that was so important you couldn't look after Isobel?" The disappointment in his voice is enough to bring me to tears.

The truth flies to my lips before I can stop it. "I was hanging out with Connor and some of his friends."

Granddad pours himself a glass of sweet tea. "I'm glad to hear that you and Connor are getting along so well, but you should have kept an eye on your sister."

"She was with Alex. I thought *he* was keeping an eye on her."

"Oh, I'll be having a talk with him too. But really, Ivy—you thought a bunch of senior baseball players were the best company for a drunk, vulnerable fifteen-year-old girl?" He raises his bushy eyebrows.

I think of all the senior boys on the baseball team. Boys like Cooper Sutton. Boys I grew up with, boys who have come over to swim off the dock and have barbecues in our backyard and eat Luisa's chocolate-chip cookies by the dozens. Boys who drive their pickup trucks around town and honk and holler at girls walking down the street. Some of Alex's friends are douche bags when it comes to girls;

Coop's a good example of that. But I don't want to believe any of them would have hurt Isobel.

Only that's not how the world works, is it?

Claire's right. I can be really naive sometimes.

"I know Alex would never take advantage of her," Granddad continues. "But I don't know about his friends, and from the look on your face, you're not so sure either. You have a sister now, Ivy, and you have a responsibility to look out for her. I know you're used to it being just you and me, and I would understand if you felt a little resentful toward Isobel for—"

"Are you serious?" I interrupt. "Do you honestly think I would have let something happen to her because I'm mad that I have to share my damn towels? I've tried! She doesn't want anything to do with me."

He fixes me with a frown. "Well, she needs you, whether she's willing to admit it or not. Don't give up on her. She's having a hard time right now."

And I'm not? What do I have to do for my feelings to be taken into consideration?

"I understand," I say tightly. "Am I grounded too, or can I go to bed?"

"Tone, Ivy," Granddad says, and waits for me to apologize. But he'd have to wait a hell of a long time, because I'm tired of apologizing when I don't mean it. I stare at him until he sighs and relents. "You're not grounded. But

I want to see you making more of an effort with Isobel, all right? This is new territory for all of us. We're all going to make mistakes. I know it wasn't our idea to keep her in the dark, but we need to work extra hard now to make amends. To earn her trust."

"I understand," I say. "Good night."

I trudge upstairs. Pass the bathroom, where I can hear Isobel throwing up.

I pause. Should I stop and—what? Offer to hold her hair?

Erica ruined everything, so now *I* have to work extra hard to prove myself.

That's the story of my life.

And I am getting goddamn sick of it.

I keep walking.

CHAPTER
SIXTEEN

GRACIE FINDS ME IN THE KITCHEN LATE THE NEXT MORNING.
"Something's wrong with Izzy," she announces. "She's
sick. I heard her throw up and she says she doesn't want
any ginger ale and I don't know what to do."

I get up from the table, where I've been reading an
awesome graphic novel, *Nimona*, that I borrowed from the
library on Abby's recommendation. I go to the fridge and
pour some ginger ale because, like it or not, Izzy needs to
hydrate. "I'm on it."

Gracie hovers. "She says her head hurts."

"I bet it does."

Grace's little face is all scrunched up with worry. Her
blond hair is pulled back into a simple ponytail, which

makes me think it's Isobel who braids her hair every morning. That softens my annoyance. "I'll take care of her. Don't worry. Why don't you go read more Fancy Nancy in the sunroom?"

Gracie beams at me. "Izzy always says when I have a problem I should tell her because she's the big sister and she'll fix it. So I knew I could tell you because now *you're* the big sister!" She throws her arms around my waist and then runs off, her bare feet pattering against the tile floors, clutching her book in one hand and her stuffed puppy in the other.

I knock lightly on their bedroom door before letting myself in. Isobel's side of the room is a mess of clothes and shoes, and she's taped posters from a few Broadway shows on the walls: *Hamilton*, *The Book of Mormon*, and *Chicago*. Isobel herself is curled up on her twin bed. She opens one eye and glares at me. "Did I say you could come in?"

"Sit up." I stride across the room and yank the curtains open.

"What the hell!" she shrieks, blinking and throwing her arm over her eyes. "Why would you *do* that?"

"You need to get up. You're freaking Gracie out. She thinks you're dying or something." Isobel sits up and I hand her the glass of ginger ale. "Drink this. Then we'll get you something to eat."

Isobel's hair is straggling out of last night's braids, and last night's mascara and eyeliner are smeared beneath her eyes. "Don't tell me *you've* gotten trashed."

"I haven't, but Alex has." I smile at the memory. "It was some dumb initiation for the baseball team freshman year. He was scared to go home and face Luisa, and Granddad was at some faculty thing, so Alex came over here and hid out. He got sick and then ended up taking a nap in the living room. I made it look like he fell asleep watching an old movie with me."

Iz takes a few tentative sips, then lies back down. "Did he get away with it?"

"Nope. We thought we were sneaky, but Luisa totally grounded him."

She groans. "Mama would never ground me. Do I really have to go to that stupid theater camp? Can't you, like, talk to Granddad for me?"

"Wouldn't do any good. He doesn't change his mind about stuff like that." I sit on Gracie's unmade bed. She has *Frozen* sheets.

"*You* didn't get in trouble," Iz complains.

"I got a lecture for letting you get drunk," I say. "Has Erica checked on you?"

"Are you kidding? No. She's barely looked at me since we found out you're our sister."

"Maybe she feels bad for lying." I stack the pile of chapter books next to Gracie's bed.

"Um, no. She just doesn't want to deal with me being mad. That's why she pawned me off on Alex last night. You think she cares whether I make friends?" Iz leans up on one elbow. "I have every right to be mad at her. And at you."

I lift my gaze to hers. "I'm sorry. I really am. I wish I'd told you the truth the day you got here."

"Well, I don't forgive you." She rolls over to face the wall.

"I guess I'll just have to live with that." I sit there for a minute, listening to her breath and the lazy whir of the ceiling fan. When it becomes obvious that she isn't going to answer me, I stand. "You can be mad at me, but don't do stupid shit like this again, okay? Gracie worries about you too much. She needs you. You're her big sister."

I close the door behind me without waiting for a response.

· · · · ·

That afternoon, Granddad takes Gracie into town with the promise of strawberry milk shakes and a new Fancy Nancy book. Erica is off God knows where, so the house is quiet. Iz came downstairs for lunch, nibbled at her turkey sandwich, and then went back upstairs for a nap. I'm sitting at the kitchen table reading *Nimona* again when Claire knocks at the back door.

"I was thinking we should go for a swim," she suggests. "We'll invite Iz. Your granddad will be happy you're spending time with her, but I'll be there as a buffer."

We have already texted about the fallout from last night. "She doesn't want to hang out with us."

Claire grins. "Maybe not with you, but she thinks I'm pretty cool." She sees me wince and her smile fades. "Are you jealous that your sister thinks I'm cool?"

"No." Claire stares at me until I relent. "Maybe a little? I'd settle for her not hating me."

"Give her time," Claire advises. "You're too nice to hate."

Nice. Likeable. That's what I want, isn't it? But sometimes having to be *nice* grates.

"You can ask her to come. I don't think she'll say yes if I'm part of the package."

"You are underestimating my powers of persuasion. Don't ever do that," Claire chides. Her dark hair is pulled back into a high, bouncy ponytail. "Go get your suit and meet Iz and me down here in five minutes."

· · · · ·

It takes fifteen, but somehow Claire convinces her. She even convinces Iz to wear a bathing suit. It's a deep-purple-and-white polka-dotted tankini and Iz looks fantastic, if a little self-conscious. She keeps a towel wrapped around her waist as we walk down to the water, while Claire strips to her black bikini right in the kitchen.

I run and dive off the dock like always. "Show-off," Claire teases like always. She wades in from the shore, wincing as every new inch of skin hits the cold water.

Iz follows Claire tentatively. "So this is where our grandmother drowned? Like, right here?" she asks. "Isn't that kind of creepy?"

I shrug. "I try not to think about it."

"Why didn't Granddad move? Why would he stay here?" she asks.

I've wondered that myself.

"He loves this house. All the history of it," I explain. "I guess he thinks more about the happy memories than the sad ones."

"I think her paintings are creepy. Pretty but creepy," Isobel declares.

"Me too," I say.

We all look up as the roar of the lawnmower gets louder. Alex is coming around the side of the carriage house on the riding mower. He's shirtless and wearing headphones and, by the looks of it, singing. I wave. He does not wave back. I shrink into myself. *Maybe he didn't see me?*

"Cold," Claire says. She gives him the finger.

Isobel takes a few more steps until she's knee deep. "Why's he mad at you?"

"It's complicated." I dunk under the water.

When I come back up, I hear: "...so he's mad that she's dating Connor. She's never had a real boyfriend before."

"You've never had a boyfriend? Mama said you were like a nun." Iz laughs—not meanly but sort of disbelievingly—and I give her a strained smile. I'm not sure how I feel about the fact that my fifteen-year-old sister's more experienced than me. "I've had three. Four if you count Josh, but that was back in sixth grade and we only held hands. Claire, do *you* have a boyfriend?"

It's Claire's turn to evade the question. "Not right now."

"Claire doesn't date," I explain. "She thinks boyfriends are too much drama."

"*Relationships* are too much drama, whether they're with boys or girls. Don't be heteronormative." Claire turns to Isobel. "I'm bi."

"Bisexual?" Isobel asks, and Claire nods. "My friend Rhiannon is too."

"Really? I don't know anyone else who's bi. Everybody around here thinks I'm just a slut." Claire sighs. "I can't wait to get away from all this small-town nonsense. I'm going to go to college in DC, so you'll have to tell me all the fun places."

"Sure. What about you, Ivy?" Iz splashes me to get my attention. "Where do you want to go to college? Harvard? Yale?"

Is that how she sees me? As some superachiever destined for the Ivy League? "Nope. Nothing that fancy. I might end up staying here. They have a good swim team and a good English program, and I could go for free since Granddad's a professor."

"Mama said Granddad's loaded," Iz says.

She's so direct. No wonder she likes Claire so much; they are kindred spirits in that regard. "We don't really have to worry about money, but most of it's not his. It belongs to the Milbourn estate, and some of it goes into a trust for me. And you and Gracie. But...I don't know. It feels kind of frivolous to spend so much money on college if I don't have to. If I want to go to grad school, that will cost a lot of money, so—"

"Grad school?" Iz grimaces. "You must really like school."

I laugh. "I do, actually. I've been thinking I might want to teach. Be a professor like Granddad." It's a newish thought, one I've shared only with Claire and Abby. Last summer I helped teach swim lessons at the Y, and even if I'm not a great writer, I love studying books, teasing out the themes, examining the characters.

"I hate school. It's so boring," Iz complains. "Like history class. Oh my God. Who cares about all those names and dates?"

"That's because most of history's been whitewashed so it's all about straight white men," Claire says. "My mom teaches a class on women's history up at the college, and it's actually really interesting. She talks about how women got the vote and birth control. I'm going to major in women's, gender, and sexuality studies at American. I'm president of our Gay-Straight Alliance at school. If you're still here in September, you should join."

Isobel freezes mid-paddle. "I'm not going to be here that long."

"Probably not," Claire says. "But if your mom goes into treatment or something…"

"Is *that* what you think is going to happen?" Isobel narrows her eyes at me. "You think Mama's going to go to rehab and Gracie will go live with Dad and I'll be stuck here? Is that why you're being so nice to me?"

"What? No. I'm being nice to you because you're my *sister*." My heart sinks. This was the longest conversation we've ever had, and okay, she made fun of me for not having a boyfriend, but it felt sort of…sisterly. Like in her own prickly Isobel kind of way, she was trying to get to know me.

"You feel sorry for me. I can tell." Isobel tugs on the bottom of her tankini. "You think Mama's going to run off on us the way she did you. Well, she's not. She wouldn't do that. She wouldn't leave us. Things got really bad before

Gracie and Dad, but she's never left me." Isobel storms out of the water and wraps a towel around herself.

"Iz, she wasn't—" Claire wades toward the shore.

"Don't defend her." Isobel glares at me again. "You're not my sister. You're just some stranger I have to live with for a while."

She stomps up to the house, passing Alex, who waves at *her*.

Claire turns to me, sympathy written all over her face. "Wow," she says. "That kid has a temper on her."

I nod. "Like mother, like daughter."

· · · · ·

Gracie is mad when she comes home and finds out that Izzy went swimming with Claire and me. She stomps around the library in her pink sandals like an adorable, inconsolable T. rex. "I want to go swimming! It's not fair! How come Mama let Izzy learn how and not me? I'm big enough to learn how to swim!" she complains.

"If your mama says no swimming, then we need to respect that," Granddad says, even though he seems to have precious little respect for the rest of Erica's rules (or lack thereof). "But maybe you and Ivy could do something special tomorrow."

Gracie brightens. "Like a special sister date?"

"Sure." My mind spins, trying to dream up something fun.

"Sometimes Mama and I have special Grace-and-Mama dates," she says. "We go get our toes painted and go to the movies, and Mama lets me put M&M's in our popcorn."

I hesitate. I can't quite picture that version of our mother. "Do she and Izzy have Iz-and-Mama dates?"

"Uh-huh. They go see musicals." Gracie grins. "So what're we going to do for our sister date?"

I think fast. Abby has off tomorrow. "Do you know how to ride a bike?"

"Yes." Gracie looks insulted at the idea that she might not. "Daddy taught me."

"Okay. How about we get my old bike out for you and ride our bikes to the park? We can have a picnic with my friend Abby and her little sister. Ella's almost the same age as you."

Gracie grins. "Can we bring ice cream cookie-wiches?"

I tweak her ponytail. "Ice cream cookie-wiches would probably melt, but we can bake cookies. Whatever kind you want."

"Peanut butter!" Gracie shrieks, and runs off to the kitchen. A minute later I hear the clatter of pots and pans as she extracts a cookie sheet from its cabinet. I like that she knows where it is. That she feels at home here already.

·····

Sunday afternoon, Grace and I ride our bikes through the side streets to the park. There is a wedding taking place down by the water. The bridesmaids are dressed in coral and the groomsmen are in gray suits, and Grace squeals with excitement when she spots the bride. I have to grab her hand and tell her she can't go closer. We set up our blue-plaid blanket and wait for Abby and Ella to arrive. Abby texts me to say they're running late. **E refused to ride his boy bike so we had to get V's old bike out of the shed & it was covered in spiders,** she explains. I've prepped Grace by telling her that Ella looks kind of like a boy but is really a girl, and she said okay.

Gracie and I amuse ourselves by making up pretend vows for the couple getting married. "I promise to love you and honor you even if you—" I begin.

"Toot!" she says, and howls with laughter.

"I promise to love and honor you even if you—"

"Eat all the cookies!"

We go on like this for a while, until I see Abby and Ella approaching. Ella is riding their sister Vanessa's pink bike, which is tricked out with a pink basket and streamers.

"Sorry, sorry," Abby says as she hops off her bike and puts down the kickstand. "Someone had to ride *this* bike and not her old one."

"It's *beautiful*," Gracie declares, running over to Ella. "Can I ride it?"

"Maybe after lunch," I suggest.

Ella studies Grace. "I like your sunglasses."

Gracie studies Ella back: her tangled shoulder-length red hair, freckles, yellow sundress, pink sneakers. "I like your sneakers."

"Pink is my favorite color," Ella says.

"Mine too," Gracie says.

"You can ride my bike now if you want," Ella decides, as though Gracie has passed a test of some kind.

"Can I, Ivy? Please?" Gracie asks.

"Go ahead. But stay away from that wedding." Gracie hops on Ella's bike, and Ella hops on Gracie's, and they ride off, fast friends.

"She didn't even blink an eye at him. *Her*," Abby says. "God, I feel so bad. I got so frustrated with Ella earlier. We were all ready to go and then she freaked out about her bike being a boy's bike because it's blue and has the Avengers on it. Like, why can't you just wear pants and ride that bike? I'm wearing pants! I like the

Avengers! But it was so important to him. *Her.* Dammit!
I keep doing that."

"You're trying," I say. "That's what's important."

Abby is quiet for a minute. "Do you think she's weird?"

"Ella?" I ask, and she nods. I pause, trying to get the
words right. "I really respect her. She's seven and she's
insisting that people treat her the way she wants to be
treated. That's incredibly brave. Braver than me. I'm
always worried about what people think."

"Me too," Abby says. "People are going to judge
her. Judge our whole family. I hate that."

I lean over and give her a hug. "I'm sorry. I know it's
hard. Has your dad come around?"

She shakes her head. "Things are pretty tense between
him and Mom. He almost didn't let us come today with
Ella wearing a dress and riding Vanessa's bike. But Mom
said to go and get the spiders off it and she'd take care of
Dad. Ty told me he agrees with Dad and can't believe
we're letting Ella call the plays."

Jesus. Trust Ty to have a sports metaphor for everything. He's not a bad guy, but he definitely has a limited
imagination. I watch Ella and Gracie for a minute.
"Look at her," I say. "She's so happy. Think of how she
was last year when your parents cut her hair and tried
to make her dress like a boy. Who cares what people
think?"

Abby leans her head on my shoulder. "You're a good big sister, Ivy."

I watch Gracie, but I'm remembering Iz's fury yesterday. "I'm trying."

CHAPTER
SEVENTEEN

DEAR MS. MILBOURN: WE ARE PLEASED TO ACCEPT YOUR POEM FOR publication in our August issue…

That's how my Monday starts off.

I let out a little "Eep!" and bounce on my bed. I did it! I'm going to have a poem published! Okay, it's just an online magazine, but it's a start. Everyone starts somewhere, right? I have to tell Granddad!

I rush downstairs, still in my pajamas. It's too early for Luisa to be here yet, but the scent of coffee wafts up the stairs. I burst into the kitchen. Granddad's already sitting at the table, reading the newspaper and drinking from his banana-yellow *World's Best Grandpa* mug. I made it for him for Father's Day at the ceramics camp he made me take the summer I was Gracie's age. It's ugly as hell and the handle is misshapen, but he still uses it all the time.

"Guess what?" I demand.

He smiles at me absently over the paper. "Good morning, Ivy."

"Good morning. Guess what! Guess, guess, guess!" I bounce on my toes.

"By the look on your face, something exciting," he muses. "But I've only just started my coffee. You'll have to tell me."

"Look!" I shove my phone at him, and he squints to read the screen. "I got a poem accepted! To be published online!"

He beams at me. "That's wonderful. I knew your persistence would pay off."

My persistence. Not my talent.

I hold on to my delight with sticky fingers. "It'll be in their August issue. Look. Ms. Reeder—that's their editor—said the imagery in the last line is 'sharp and evocative'!"

"Good imagery is important in poetry." He takes another sip of coffee. "When do I get to read it?"

I hesitate. "When it's published?" I wonder if it's obvious that the poem is about me wanting to hold hands with Connor. Wanting to do more than hold hands. I blush, suddenly mortified at the thought of strangers reading it. Worse, of people I *know* reading it. Granddad. Amelia and the other English professors up at the college. Judy and Susan down at the Book Addict. Mrs. Summers... Oh Jesus. Granddad will share the link all over town. Knowing him, he'll print copies and hand them out. And everyone will think, *He's so proud of that girl*, but...

I only thought as far as getting an acceptance. My poems are a way to put all my scrambled-egg feelings down on paper. There's a reason I don't go letting everyone read them; they're private. I submitted this one on impulse, trying to prove a point. Now that I succeeded, what comes next? Granddad won't be content with one poem. One poem could be a fluke. Maybe *everybody* has one good poem in them.

But if I keep reading, keep writing, surely I'll improve. I just have to make time for it in between swimming and volunteering at the library and working on the Dorothea project and French homework and spending time with Connor and trying to be a good sister to Isobel and Grace and having fun with Claire and Abby and... I feel dazed thinking about it all. And that's before school even starts.

"We'll have to celebrate today and again in August when it's published," Granddad says. "What do you think about banana chocolate-chip pancakes for breakfast?"

That's my traditional birthday breakfast. Has been since I was little. I hear a door open upstairs and wonder fleetingly if Erica even knows what Gracie and Iz's favorite breakfasts are.

Granddad is staring at me expectantly.

"That sounds perfect. I can't wait to tell Luisa!" She'll be so excited. Iz sleeps late, but Gracie will be up soon and maybe the four of us can have pancakes together. I cross my fingers behind my back that Erica will sleep in and not ruin everything with her presence.

"Aren't you glad I kept at you to submit something?" Granddad asks.

"I am." But I get a sinking feeling in my stomach. Is my success about me or him?

"Why don't I ask Eleanor to take a look at a couple of your other poems? Give you some feedback?" he suggests. "If you revise with her help, I bet you'll have a better chance at getting more work accepted."

Eleanor is another one of the professors up at the college; she teaches freshman comp, Poetry I and Poetry II, and a special topics class on poetry of the Harlem Renaissance that Connor is really excited to take this fall. She's the real deal, with a couple of chapbooks and poems published in various journals and magazines.

"Um, that's okay." *More.* Already, he's thinking *more* and *next.* What have I gotten myself into?

"It wouldn't be any trouble. I'm sure she'd be happy to do it." Granddad gets up to fetch himself another cup of coffee, and I slump in my seat like someone's let all the helium out of me. "I'll email her about it this afternoon and she—"

"I said *no*!"

Granddad startles and spills his coffee. "Ivy, there's no need to snap."

I take a deep breath. "I'm sorry. Can we just take a minute and celebrate this? Please? I don't have any other poems that are ready to share."

He frowns, sitting down and straightening his paper with a rustle. "I thought that was our agreement, honey, that you'd keep working on your poetry this summer and submit several poems."

Several. Not just one. The chant begins in my head: not enough, not enough, *never* enough.

"That was our agreement *before* I took on the Dorothea project and that French class. Before I had two sisters to look after."

"I do appreciate that you made time for Grace and Isobel this weekend," Granddad says slowly. There's a *but* in his voice. He doesn't come right out with it, just leaves me with that inadequate feeling hanging over me like a thundercloud. He checks his watch. "You better get going or you're going to be late."

"I thought maybe I'd skip the pool today so I can tell Luisa as soon as she gets here?" I hate that I phrase it like a question, like I'm asking for permission.

"Now, Ivy, don't go getting lazy on me," he chides.

Lazy? Seriously? "It's summer! I thought we were going to celebrate! One morning off won't kill me."

"It might not kill you, but it won't help you get ahead of that girl from Salisbury either," he says, and I guess there is some truth to that. "Go on, now. We'll have pancakes waiting when you get back."

I could argue. Erica would.

Or flat-out refuse. Iz would.

But that's not me. Never has been.

·····

I run into Charlotte Wu, Alex's Halloween party hookup and my swim teammate/rival, as I'm leaving the pool. We see each other here sometimes, me leaving the women's locker room as she arrives for the last hour of free swim. Usually she ignores me or gives me a halfhearted wave, but today she bounces right over. "Hey, Ivy! Did you have fun at the bonfire Friday night?"

I nod, mystified by her sudden friendliness. I don't even remember seeing her at the party, but I was pretty preoccupied. "Yeah, it was fun." Not as much fun as if I hadn't had to leave early and cart Iz home. I'd envisioned the night ending with Connor walking me home and some seriously swoony good night kisses, not a lecture from Granddad and the sounds of my sister vomiting.

"Who was the guy you came with?" Charlotte asks.

Ah. She's not being friendly; she's being nosy. "My boyfriend." I blush, testing out the word, still shiny-penny new. "Connor."

She grins. "He's really cute. Is he a student here?"

I nod, pulling my bag out of my locker. "A sophomore."

"Cool." She fiddles with the strap on her blue swimsuit, pretending nonchalance. Badly. "So, you and Alex…?"

"Just friends. We were always just friends," I tell her, and her resulting smile could power the whole swim center.

"Oh. I mean, I know he brought your sister to the party. Isobel, right? She seems really sweet," Charlotte says, and I almost laugh because of all the ways I'd describe Iz, "sweet" is not among them. "Katie said that was just a favor though. Is he seeing anybody?"

"Not that I know of. We haven't been hanging out much lately." Which is an understatement, but his request for space is none of Charlotte's business. How could I have missed her massive crush on Alex? It's not like she's trying real hard to hide it. Or maybe that's only now that she knows I'm not a rival for his affection.

"Oh. That's too bad." She shifts from foot to foot. "I guess you're pretty busy with your new sisters. I mean, new to town. I mean…" She winces. "I was there the other day when your mom—? I can't believe she kept them away from you all this time. That sucks. My little sisters are a pain, but I don't know what I'd do without them."

I nod. I've seen Charlotte's sisters in the stands, cheering her on at swim meets. Carrie is going be a freshman this year, and Charlotte said she might try out for our team. I wonder what clubs Iz would join, if she were staying long enough to start school in September. Would she try out for the fall play? Abby says they're doing *The Crucible*. Would Gracie and Iz come with Granddad to my swim meets and cheer for me?

Before Erica arrived—before I met Gracie and Iz—I thought them staying till September would be the worst. Now I'm starting to dread the day they leave. I'd even be willing to put up with Erica to keep my sisters in town. When did that change?

"Okay, well, I'd better get in there before free swim ends. See you!" Charlotte says, and I realize I've been quiet for a long time.

"See you," I echo.

I walk back through campus slowly in the early-morning heat, keeping to the redbrick paths. The college was founded back in the 1780s—one of the first colleges in the new nation—and the buildings have mostly kept that redbrick-colonial feel. The sweet scent of freshly mown grass fills the air. A few groundskeepers are edging the sidewalks and mowing the lawn where the all-campus picnics are held. Besides the whine of the lawnmower and the buzz of the Weedwacker, it's quiet. No students rushing to the dining hall to grab breakfast or stumbling bleary-eyed to early-morning classes.

It's so pretty here. And so familiar. When I was little and Luisa was sick or on vacation, Granddad would tote me with him to his office. I grew up surrounded by his framed diplomas and shelves of leather-bound books, reading quietly in the corner while he had office hours. I'd come with him to pick up papers and play with the magnetic poetry on the secretary's filing cabinet. I ate hot dogs with Claire and the other faculty kids during reunion weekend picnics. The college is home as much as Cecil is. As much as Granddad and Alex and Luisa are.

I cross the street that separates campus from town and think back to Charlotte. I wonder how I'd feel about her and Alex dating. Just a few weeks ago, Alex having a girlfriend would have freaked me out. Would his girlfriend be jealous of me and all the time we spend together? Would he bail on our movie nights and family croquet games to go out with her instead?

Now I just miss my friend. The last week has been hard. Really hard. It would have been easier with Alex there, popping in and out of the kitchen to sneak peanut butter cookies from Gracie and me, staying for supper once or twice and making everybody laugh, lightening the ever-present tension.

He was there the night they arrived. Got to see firsthand how awful Erica was. He knows how much I need him right now.

The more I walk, the angrier I get.

Claire's right. I've needed Alex in the last week, and he ghosted on me. I understand that I hurt him—but he's the one who totally shut me out because I got a boyfriend, not the other way around. I never got mad when he kissed other girls!

When I get home, instead of making my way into the kitchen for my celebratory breakfast, I head to the carriage house instead. The small brick building is nestled between two shady old oak trees. The front door is open and I can hear Alex's music blaring, so I knock on the wooden part of the screen door. It feels strange not to call out and go right in. When I was little, I was in and out of this house as much as Alex was in and out of mine.

But we aren't little kids anymore. Things change.

The music turns off and Alex comes to the door, clad only in a pair of red shorts. When he sees it's me, his mouth tilts into a scowl. "What do you want, Ivy?"

"To talk to you." I don't wait for him to invite me in, because it's pretty apparent he isn't going to. I pull open the screen door.

"It would have been hard for me if you were dating Charlotte Wu—" I start.

"What are you talking about? I'm not dating Charlotte." Alex leans over the back of the couch, picks up a white T-shirt, and pulls it on.

"If you were though. If you'd started dating her at Halloween after the two of you hooked up, I would have been jealous, and I would have been worried about how it would change our friendship. But I wouldn't have stopped being your friend. I wouldn't have *abandoned* you."

Alex rolls his eyes. "Abandon? That's a little dramatic, Ivy."

"Well, that's how it feels." I pace the hardwood floor between the front windows. I remember when Luisa ripped out the ugly, orange shag carpet and refinished the floors underneath. "I needed you this week. You know how freaked out I was about my mother coming back. It's been a nightmare. She drinks too much, and she fights with everybody in sight. She and Granddad can't go ten minutes in the same room without an argument. Half the time it's about me. Did you hear about the scene she made at Java Jim's?"

Alex nods, his lips pressed into a thin line.

"So you heard, but you didn't come by and see if I was okay? She called me a bitch in front of everybody! Told me it would be all my fault if Gracie and Iz get separated. She told me I'm the kind of girl who people leave."

My voice wobbles on that last one. Alex reaches out a hand, then lets it fall halfway between us. "I didn't know."

"Because you didn't ask!" I throw my hands in the air. "You're supposed to be my best friend, and you haven't been there for me at all."

He leans a hip against the couch. "Why do you need me? You have Claire and Abby. And Connor."

"They're not *you*." I struggle to find the right words. "They don't live here. They don't know Granddad—not the way you know him, because he raised you too. They don't know how weird it is, walking in and hearing the TV on all the time, or finding empty wine bottles in the trash, or having to eat in the dining room because we can't all fit around the kitchen table. I know you don't want me to think of you as family, but I do. It might not be in the way you want, but I love you, Alex, and I need you. Having a boyfriend doesn't change that."

There's a long silence.

"It does," Alex says finally, rubbing a hand over his stubbly jaw. "For me, it does. I don't want to be your brother, Ivy. I meant what I said before. I need some space. It's not forever."

"So my feelings don't matter? I don't get a say in this?" I ask. He doesn't meet my eyes, just shrugs. The utter carelessness of the gesture makes me furious. "Fine. Take your space. But you can't disappear when all these huge things are happening and then come back in a week or a month and expect that our friendship will be the same. Because it won't."

"Whatever," he says. Like he can throw fifteen years of friendship right out the window. Like my feelings *don't* matter. All that matters to him is that there's another boy in my life, and he's punishing me for it.

"*Whatever?*" I echo. "Seriously? Go to hell."

I stomp out of the house, letting the screen door bang shut behind me. I don't know how I expected that to go—for him to apologize? To care that he's hurt me? To see that there's room for both him and Connor in my life?

I make my way to the main house, apologies on my lips for being late. But no one is there. A plate of cold banana chocolate-chip pancakes sits on the counter with a note from Granddad explaining that he's sorry he missed me, but he had to register Isobel for her first day of theater camp and then he's taking Gracie for a playdate with Professor Campbell's daughter. Luisa added a PS that she had to run out to the market but she'll be back soon.

I sink into a chair and prop my chin in my hands, blinking back tears.

So much for my special celebration.

I'm still pushing cold pancakes around my plate when

Connor rings the doorbell. He's a little early for work. He must notice that Granddad's car isn't in the driveway because he bends down and kisses me right there on the front porch.

"Good morning," he says.

I muster up a smile. "Hi."

"So what's the exciting news?" he asks as I lead the way to the library.

I forgot that I texted him a hint. It doesn't even feel worth celebrating anymore.

"That poem I submitted was accepted."

"What? That's fantastic!" He takes in my Eeyore face. "Isn't it? What's wrong?"

"Nothing. I just… I thought Granddad would be more excited." I drop into Granddad's big leather recliner. Connor sets his bag and his coffee down and sits on the edge of the couch. "It's dumb, but I guess I expected a magical moment where he'd say he was proud of me and I'd stop feeling so *inadequate*."

"You are not inadequate." Connor reaches out and traces his thumb over my ankle. Even in my despondency, his touch makes my heart race. "Can I read it? The poem? You never told me what it was about."

I play with the frayed edge of my red shorts. "Well, it's kind of about you."

He grins. "Now I'm *really* curious."

I grab my phone and pull up the poem in my email. "Here. Just don't tell me if it's terrible, okay?"

"I'm sure it's not terrible," he says.

I get up, pacing back and forth, back and forth, in front of the french doors.

After a minute, I look over at him. It's not a very long poem. Why isn't he saying anything?

"When did you write this?" he asks.

My heart races at the strain in his voice. "Last week. That day we had lunch. What's wrong?"

"Ivy…" he starts, then trails off. He stands, putting my phone down on the coffee table.

"Is it terrible? It's terrible, isn't it?"

"It's not terrible. It's just… The last line—" Connor goes to the bookshelf and retrieves Dorothea's first journal from the bottom shelf. He pages through it, his brow furrowed. "Ivy, that last line isn't yours."

"What do you mean, *not mine*?" Even though I'm standing in the middle of a patch of sunshine, I feel icy cold.

He holds the journal out to me, pointing to Dorothea's words spiraling across the page in faded blue ink. I take it from him with a sinking stomach and read. There, at the bottom, Dorothea talks about Robert Moudowney. About sitting across from him at a picnic in the town square and wanting so badly for him to take her hand.

And she uses my words.

Except, they were her words first.

I fumble and Connor catches the journal before it hits the floor.

"No. I didn't…" I feel like I'm going to throw up. I can't meet his eyes. Instead, I stare at the portrait of Dorothea above the mantel. She looks unbearably smug in her little gloves and smart navy shirtdress and neat, pin-curled hair. *She* would never make this kind of mistake. "I thought I made it up. I didn't realize—"

"It was an accident," Connor says. "It's just that one line. I only remembered because the phrase really stuck with me. It was such a great image."

"The editor said it was 'sharp and evocative.' That's what she liked best about the poem. The part—the part that wasn't really mine." I bury my face in my hands. "I am so stupid."

"Hey." Connor takes my hands and moves them away from my face. "Don't beat yourself up. It was an honest mistake. At least we caught it before publication. You can still pull the poem."

Pull the poem. Of course. Otherwise it'd be plagiarism.

But that means I'll have to tell Granddad what happened. What I accidentally did. Whatever pride he mustered up for my persistence—my effort, if not my talent—will disappear. I cheated. I didn't mean to, but I did.

"He'll be so disappointed," I whisper. "And he'll be right. I'm not a poet. I'm not *anything*."

"Ivy, I have to ask. Do you *want* to be a poet? Are you doing this for you or for him?"

I don't answer.

Connor tips my chin up with one finger until I have to meet his pretty, golden eyes. "I see you jumping through hoops to try to earn his approval, to measure up to some Milbourn ideal, and it's making you hate yourself. Is it really worth it?"

"I can answer that."

We both whirl around at the low, smoky voice. Erica. She strides into the room, her spiky blond hair still wet from the shower, her makeup perfectly applied—the slash of red lipstick, the cat's-eye black eyeliner. She's dressed in a long, striped black-and-gray tunic and black capris, her hands laden with silver rings and a silver necklace draped around her throat. She looks sleek and powerful, like some elegant cat waiting to pounce.

"Sorry for interrupting," she says with a smile that's not sorry at all.

CHAPTER
EIGHTEEN

"Connor, this is Erica. Erica, Connor."

Erica takes one look at us—at the distance between us, or lack thereof—and taps her long, taupe fingernails against her pointy chin. "So *you're* the reason she's not dating the housekeeper's kid."

"His name is Alex," I say through gritted teeth, "and I'm not dating him because he's like my brother. But yes, Connor is my boyfriend. And one of Granddad's students. We're working together to—"

"Archive Dorothea's journals. I heard." Erica flutters a hand at the bookshelves, her silver rings catching the sunlight. "If it were up to me, I'd set the damn things on fire; I'm that sick of hearing her name." She gives a rich, throaty laugh as Connor's jaw drops in horror. "Oh, look at you. You *are* one of Dad's disciples. Are you dating Ivy for extra credit?"

Because that's the only reason a boy like him—brilliant, ambitious, gorgeous—would ever date me.

Logically I know it's not true. Connor wouldn't use me like that. But somehow I don't trust *myself* to—what, exactly? Be the kind of girl people won't leave?

The fight with Alex sticks in my head. In my throat, an ever-present ache. In a spot below my ribs, caught between fury and tears. He's my oldest friend. He knows me better than anyone—or used to. How could he cut me out of his life so easily, like chopping off a bad limb?

Connor takes my hand. "I don't care what her last name is."

"Good. I know his students idolize him, but my father is not perfect. Far from it. The man is so haunted by his own mediocrity that he's become a vampire feeding off our talents. A… What are they called? A succubus. Are there male succubuses?"

"Succubi," I correct automatically. "And that's not true. He just wants me to be my best."

"Really? Is your best ever good enough?" Erica sits on the couch, crossing one slim, tanned leg over the other. "'Cause mine never was."

I'm silent, struck by this, and she continues. "I wonder

what you've been told. Let me guess: how reckless I am,
how selfish. Not just for leaving, but for throwing away the
talent God gave me. I think maybe it's time you heard the
story from my point of view, Ivy."

I still don't like the way my name sounds in her mouth.

"Why, so I can hear what a monster Granddad is? No
thank you." I straighten my shoulders. Pretend that part of
me isn't hanging on her every word.

Erica ignores what I want, like always. "He's a vain,
egotistical old bastard and he'll destroy you if you let him.
He cares more about this family's precious reputation than
your happiness. He'll take the thing you love most, the
thing that makes you *yourself*, and he'll push and he'll push
until you can't remember why you ever loved it in the
first place. For me it was singing. One solo in the concert?
Why not two? It's never good enough, and it's always
your fault for not doing more or better. It's damn near
impossible to please him, and you'll only twist yourself
into knots trying."

I don't want to hear this. But as unkind as her words are,
they're also sort of…true.

I look to Connor, but he's quiet. He won't step in and
speak for me like Granddad would. He won't sling an arm
around me and make a joke like Alex would. But he's here.
Listening. Letting me figure things out. Trusting that I
can—that I am smart enough, capable enough on my own.

"Is that why you quit singing?" I ask my mother.

"I didn't quit singing. I quit the school chorus and the church chorus and the town chorus and the voice lessons." Erica eyes the open french doors, then pulls out a pack of cigarettes and a lighter. Granddad would have a fit about her smoking in the house, especially here, with Grandmother's paintings and Dorothea's portrait and first editions. You don't smoke in a museum full of precious artifacts. "Some friends and I had a band, and we were pretty good. We got some gigs playing at parties for beer or weed, that kind of thing. It was fun. But it wasn't impressive enough."

"Or maybe," I suggest, "it was the beer and weed he had a problem with."

Erica narrows her eyes and blows a plume of smoke in my direction. "You are a judgmental little thing, aren't you? You must get that from him. I'm trying to *help* you, kid."

Jesus, could she be any more patronizing?

"Since when do you give a damn about me?" I pull away from Connor and stalk closer to her. For once I'm grateful for my height. I like the way I tower over her. It makes me feel powerful. "It's a little late for motherly advice, don't you think?"

"Maybe." She ashes her cigarette onto a pretty tile coaster that Amelia gave us, a souvenir from a trip to Madrid. "But I don't want you making yourself sick like I did. You know what I weighed after Mama died?

Ninety-four pounds. And what was Dad worried about? What people would *think!*"

I remember the picture of her at the English department Christmas party, six months before Grandmother died: already rail thin, her long limbs poking out of the black velvet dress that swallowed her up. There aren't any photos of her at her high school graduation or the summer afterward or pregnant with me. Nowhere in the house. I've looked.

I remember Granddad praising my healthy appetite. *I can't abide girls who pick at their food.*

But I also remember Isobel slumped at the kitchen table, staring miserably into her bowl of grapefruit. That's not Granddad. That's all Erica.

"I don't think I'm the kid you need to have the eating disorder talk with."

"Iz?" Erica shakes her head. "She's fine. She could stand to lose a couple pounds and get off her ass instead of being on her phone all the time. She didn't grow up with all these expectations. You're the one wound up tighter than a tick. I know a miserable Milbourn girl when I see one, and you're headed for a meltdown."

Ready for a meltdown? Me? I am not the type of girl who melts down.

"That's ridiculous. I'm not miserable," I scoff. "I'm fine."

But it doesn't sound convincing. Not even to me.

"Are you?" It's Connor who asks, not Erica.

I can't believe he's siding with her. I whirl on him and he takes a step back.

"Look, maybe I should go," he says.

"No, I'll go." Erica rises and saunters toward the door. She pauses. "You need to get the hell out of this town. You're a smart girl, right? Good at school. I never was. You want to go to college, go somewhere else. No one out in the world cares that you're a Milbourn. They don't even know what a Milbourn is."

"That's your advice? To run away?" I snap. "Leave my family like you did?"

"You'll come back," she says. "Holidays. School breaks. Vacations. You don't owe him any more than that. Dad's not a saint for you to devote your life to."

"I never said he was a saint, but he's the one who *stayed*. He raised me. He *loved* me."

There's a look on her face that I've never seen before. Regret? Guilt? Whatever it is, it doesn't last. She walks away, and a minute later I hear the fridge opening. Probably time for her morning Bloody Mary.

I go stand in front of the french doors, trying to catch the breeze coming in off the Bay. The air is suffocating. It feels more like August than mid-June. "Don't you ever take her side again. That was not okay."

"I'm on *your* side. Always," Connor says. "But I'm not sure Erica's the enemy here."

"Are you kidding me? She straight up said she doesn't care about me or my feelings. I don't know where this urge to give motherly advice came from, but it's not because she wants what's best for me. She just wants to stick it to Granddad."

"What if sticking it to him *is* what's best for you?" Connor suggests. I open my mouth to protest and he puts up an ink-stained hand, forestalling my argument. "I don't believe that the Professor's half as bad as what she said. But what do you think will happen when you tell him you have to pull the poem? If you tell him that you don't want to be a poet? What is the worst possible outcome?"

"He'll think I'm like her." I whisper it like the curse it is. "That I'm selfish."

"Because you made a mistake? Because you don't want to live your life to please someone else?" Connor shakes his head. "Ivy, that's not selfish."

My heart is racing like I've been swimming long distance. Sweat pools at the small of my back and I sweep my hair into a ponytail. "You don't know what it's like to be part of this family, Connor."

He sips his iced coffee and watches me. "No, I don't. But every family comes with its own expectations. I didn't play sports. Didn't want to study business or accounting. I was never popular, not the way my sister is. You have to figure out who you are away from your family, and if you can't do that here in Cecil—"

"You don't understand."

He shrugs. "Maybe I don't. But maybe your mother does. She can be a jerk and still have some insight on this, you know? She grew up here, in the same house, with the same man."

"He's a good man," I say.

"I know. He's given me some incredible opportunities. But if he's pushing you so hard that you're about to break—"

"I'm not!" I prop my hands on my hips. "I'm not the kind of girl who breaks."

Connor shrugs again. "Everybody breaks at some point. It's how you patch yourself up that counts. If he's trying not to make the same mistakes with you that he made with your mother, maybe he doesn't realize how hard he's pushing you. Maybe it's not about you at all. It sure as hell isn't because you're inherently flawed."

But I am. I feel like I am.

Connor moves toward me slowly, like I'm some wounded animal he might scare off. I hate that he sees me being so insecure. I want him to see me as strong and confident and clever. But as he wraps me in his arms and holds me close, I feel like I can be all of those things.

"Just think about it, okay?" he asks. "Think about what *you* want. You, not your granddad. What would you do if you weren't a Milbourn?"

But I can't even imagine that.

. . . . .

That evening, after supper, Granddad and I walk into town for an open mic night at Java Jim's. Connor helped organize it and he's going to read two new poems. When Granddad heard that, he decided to come support his star student. Which puts me in the awkward position of pretending that Connor and I are just friends.

I guess, technically, I put *myself* in that position.

It's nice to be out of the house though. When we left, Erica and Gracie were watching a movie in the living room and Iz was sulking upstairs. She was not a fan of the first day of theater camp. She called Miss Saundra a pretentious asshole and Granddad threatened to extend her grounding. It made me laugh though. I tried theater camp the summer I was ten, at Granddad's insistence. I had major stage fright, and Miss Saundra's constant barking to "e-nun-ci-ate" did not help matters. I spent most of my time painting sets.

Granddad pushes open the door to Java Jim's and we're greeted by a blast of air-conditioning, followed by the scents of espresso beans and chocolate. The couches and chairs at the front have been shifted to create a small performance space. Connor's coworker Katrina is perched on a stool, a mic in front of her, her guitar across her lap. With her short, ivory lace dress and bright-pink hair and nose ring, she totally rocks the quirky singer-songwriter look. Peyton Cavanaugh, a girl from my class, is sitting on one couch with two of her friends, nervously clutching a black-and-white composition notebook. I don't recognize the girls on the other couch. Maybe they go to the college?

Connor's going to be thrilled with the turnout. The tables against the brick wall are filled with people chatting over iced lattes. I spot him at the end of the line, talking with Jay and Josh as they wait to order drinks. Connor's talking with his hands, shifting from foot to foot. I wonder if he's nervous.

Granddad hesitates as we pass the clipboard with the sign-up sheet. "Are you sure you don't want to read your poem?"

"Very." My voice is curt.

"It would be good practice," he wheedles, and ghosts of departmental Christmas parties past come parading through my memory. I was too young then for Granddad to take my reluctance seriously. He always chalked it up to stage fright.

"I would really prefer not to," I say.

"Maybe next week? You could practice reading it out loud to me first."

His voice is so hopeful. Jesus, I hate disappointing him. "Maybe," I agree, though I know I am just prolonging the inevitable. I have to tell him about the poem.

Two women leave, grumbling about the noise, and Granddad snags the now-open table along the wall. "Decaf?" I ask, and he nods, handing me a rumpled ten-dollar bill.

Connor grins when he sees me. I'm wearing red shorts and a black tank top printed with ladybugs, with my hair in two braids courtesy of Gracie. I worried it looked too childish but didn't have the heart to take the braids out. Considering the way Connor's eyes trail over me, I guess I look okay. I squeeze his forearm in greeting, but it's hard not to kiss him. His mouth is just so kissable.

The rest of him looks pretty kissable too. He's wearing jeans and a black T-shirt that hugs his broad shoulders and skims the muscles of his chest. His ink trails out from beneath the sleeve of his shirt and curves over the smooth, brown skin of his forearm. I let my hand linger there, my thumb tracing the Langston Hughes quote. He seems to relax a little beneath my touch.

"I'm really glad you're here," he confesses, and I melt. "I'm nervous."

"I wouldn't miss it. You're going to be amazing," I say.

Katrina welcomes everyone, thanks Java Jim's for hosting us, urges us to tip the baristas generously, and begins to sing. Connor offers to save me a place on the window seat with him and Josh and Jay, but I decline. Better to sit with Granddad. Easier to keep my hands to myself.

I brush a kiss over Connor's cheek. "Break a leg."

"What about me?" Jay pouts.

"I didn't know you were performing!" I kiss him on the cheek too. "What about you, Josh?"

"Uh, no." Josh looks horror-struck. "I'm just here for moral support."

"Me too," I say, and we chat about our weekends while we get our drinks. When I get back to my seat, Granddad's doing the crossword puzzle in the newspaper while he listens to Katrina. Jay's up next, and as he performs a spoken-word piece about growing up in Baltimore in a rough neighborhood, Granddad puts down his pen.

Jay's words have a quick, beautiful cadence to them, and the way he performs from memory—the rhythm and flow of it, the change from soft and thoughtful to driving and passionate—is powerful. When he's finished, everyone applauds like mad and Jay gives a big theatrical bow. Then he returns to his seat next to Connor, who claps him on the back and grins. I love that there doesn't seem to be any competition between them.

Peyton Cavanaugh goes next. She reads a poem that seems like it might be about being a lesbian. There are definitely she-her pronouns involved. Her voice wavers at first and she holds her notebook with shaking hands, but as she reads, she finds her rhythm and relaxes into it. The poem itself is not very good, but presumably it's hers and not her dead great-grandmother's, so yay for her being brave enough to get up and read it. Her friends clap and whistle when she's finished, and Peyton looks proud of herself.

Then it's Connor's turn. He adjusts the mic and props his Moleskine on the music stand. I know he's nervous, but it doesn't show. He has a natural stage presence; his low voice commands attention. The whole coffee shop hushes—the clink of glasses, the hiss of the steamer, the chatter at the back of the store—as everyone listens.

He reads about the power of naming things, about being afraid to lose his memories. The images that he paints are beautiful. One is of a girl on a bench in a yellow dress, and oh my God, that's *me*. My pulse dances as he meets my eyes. It feels like everyone else in the room disappears for a minute, and I know we're both remembering our first kiss down by the water.

I dart a quick look at Granddad, wondering if he's noticed.

But Granddad is watching Connor, his face full of pride.

Has he ever looked at me like that? Pure proud, without wanting *more* and *better* and *next*?

As Connor begins his second poem, Professor Paquin comes in. My heart sinks. If she sees us—and how could she not? Java Jim's is not that big—and she and Granddad get to talking, there is no way on earth my poem won't come up.

I wish I'd been brave enough to talk to Granddad before

we came here. To tell him about the poem. To tell him about Connor and me.

Connor recites the second poem like he was born to do this. He's perfectly at ease behind the mic and in his own skin. I know he's struggled to get there, but you could never tell from watching him. He varies his volume and speed, and he has the audience utterly enthralled. The college girls on the couch are practically swooning, and I can't blame them. Watching someone do the thing they love most is attractive. Really attractive.

When Connor finishes, Granddad claps longest and loudest. "Such mature themes for his age," he says to me. "I told you, didn't I, Ivy? He's very promising."

I nod, jealousy a thorn in my throat. Connor's my boyfriend. I should feel proud. But I would give anything to have that kind of talent.

There's a break while Katrina encourages people to sign up for the next set. Music plays over the speakers. Connor starts toward us, but he and Jay are mobbed by the college girls. All three of the girls are pretty hipsters. The petite brunette with blue streaks in her hair puts a hand on Connor's forearm, smiling up at him, and I sort of want to break her arm off.

If I'd told Granddad that Connor and I were dating, Connor would be holding my hand right now and these girls would not be flirting with him. This is my own stupid fault. I wait for Connor to excuse himself and make his way across the room to us, but he's talking, his hands waving animatedly, that big, goofy grin on his face, while the girls ply him and Jay with compliments.

Well-deserved compliments.

A wave of self-loathing breaks over me. I will never be the one up there with people clapping and whispering about how good I am because I'm a liar and a cheat and a nobody. Connor wrote me into a poem. Any other girl would be dazed with happiness. What is wrong with me?

Professor Paquin makes her way to our table. She's tall with brown skin and curly hair and a ton of energy despite having a toddler at home. "George!" she says. "Ivy! How are you? I'm sorry I didn't get here sooner. Maya refused to go to sleep."

"We're doing very well. Ivy, tell Eleanor your news!" Granddad doesn't waste any time.

"Oh, it's really not a big deal." I shift awkwardly in my chair.

"She's being modest. She had a poem accepted for publication in an online magazine!" Granddad brags. "The first of many, I'm sure."

He means well. But it doesn't feel like pride; it feels like pressure.

"Oh, that's fantastic! Congratulations, Ivy," Eleanor says.

"Thank you," I reply through gritted teeth, trying to muster a smile.

"We'll see if next week we can't get her up there reading some of her work." Granddad sips his coffee. "Do you think you'd have time to look at some of her poems? Sit down with her and give her some constructive criticism?"

Eleanor smiles. "Of course. I'd be happy to. I love working with young poets to hone their voices."

"I'm not a poet." My voice is a little too loud, but I told him no. I specifically said I didn't have anything else to share. That I didn't *want* to share it. When will he hear me?

"Everyone starts somewhere, Ivy," Granddad assures me.

"It's really no trouble," Eleanor adds.

I know I should wait until we get home. But the words spill out.

"The poem's not mine. Not the best part, the line the editor really liked. I plagiarized it." I stare down at the pretty tiled table, at my half-empty iced tea, *anything* not to see the disappointment on their faces. "I didn't mean to, but I'd been reading Dorothea's journals and that last phrase—I didn't realize it wasn't mine until today. I'm pulling the poem."

Granddad lays a hand on my arm. "Ivy, sweetheart, it's okay. It was an accident. There will be other poems."

"No. There won't." My voice is quiet but firm. "I'm not a poet like Connor or Jay or Dorothea. I don't know what my calling is, or if I even have one. I'm sorry. I know that's what you want for me. I'm sorry that I can't be what you want me to be." I stand, still avoiding Granddad's eyes. I catch a glimpse of Eleanor's face, the pity written all over it. "Excuse me. I don't feel very well. I'm going to go home."

"Sweetheart, wait," Granddad says. "I'll walk with you. Let's talk about this."

"No. Please. I don't want to talk about it anymore tonight. Stay. I know it means a lot to Connor that you're here." I'm already moving toward the door.

Connor breaks away from his fans to intercept me. "Hey, where are you going?"

"Home." My voice is sharp. "I'm sorry. You were amazing. I just—I can't do this right now."

Connor steps in front of me. "Can't do what? Did you tell the Professor about the poem? If you wait a minute, I'll walk you home."

I point to the sunshine outside. "It's eight o'clock. I'm perfectly capable of walking myself home. I don't want to ruin your big night. Go back to your fan club."

"Ivy. Hey. Are you mad at me? Did I do something wrong?"

"No. I just need to be by myself right now."

And Connor—the one person I don't want to listen to me—does. He lets me go.

CHAPTER
NINETEEN

I WALK BACK THROUGH TOWN AS THE SHADOWS ARE LENGTHENING into dusk. Fireflies wink in and out of view around me, and the air carries the scent of grilled steaks and burgers. Neighbors wave from their front porches as they sip wine or pull their dogs aside to let me pass on the narrow brick sidewalk.

I love Cecil. It's all I've ever known. I'm intimately acquainted with all its corners and quirks, with the unspoken rules of how things are done.

Over on Water Street, Susan from the Book Addict is in her front yard, spraying the pink roses that push right up against her wrought-iron fence. "Hi, Ivy!"

"Hi, Susan. Those roses are real pretty," I say.

She tucks a strand of white hair behind her ear. "Thank you, honey. You out for a walk? Nice night now that it's cooled down some."

"Just heading home. I was at the open mic night down at Java Jim's," I explain.

"Oh, that's right. I saw the flyer." She smiles at me conspiratorially. "That boyfriend of yours works there, doesn't he?"

I shake my head, both impressed and exasperated. Connor and I have been on *one* date. To a party filled with people a third her age. "He does, yes."

Susan moves on to the next rosebush. "You have a good night, Ivy."

"You too." I'm thankful she has the tact not to mention the scene in the store the other day.

What would it be like to live in a place where everyone doesn't know my business, doesn't feel perfectly at home prying into my family troubles or my love life? What would it be like to walk down a busy city street and have to consult a map for directions? To pass perfect strangers who don't know my name and entire family tree?

It seems like it could get real lonely...but it could also be pretty freeing.

I could do whatever I wanted. Dye my hair pink like Katrina and buy those over-the-knee black leather boots Claire has that Eli—Ella—calls her "superhero shoes" and Granddad says look like something a streetwalker would wear. I could read all the romance novels I want right out in public. (I currently hide them on my Kindle so Granddad won't see and judge.) I'd flat-out refuse to eat celery because I think it's a ridiculous vegetable. Watch nothing but old black-and-white movies and BBC period dramas without Alex complaining that there aren't enough explosions. I'd take classes in psychology and film and history because the world is big and interesting—and why the hell not.

I'd still swim. I know that bone deep. I might compete for Granddad, but I swim for me. I'd still wear sundresses and quirky T-shirts with robots or ladybugs on them. I'd bake pies using Luisa's tips for the perfect crust, but I wouldn't worry if the lattice top wasn't perfectly symmetrical. And the only art classes I'd take would be those "paint and sip" nights where everybody drinks cheap wine and tries to paint trees.

Letting myself daydream like this is kind of terrifying because it means I have choices.

I do. I might not always feel like it, but I do.

The house is quiet when I let myself in through the front door. Erica's car is still in the driveway, but the living room is empty. She and Gracie have turned off their movie. Bottles of nail polish and Q-tips sit abandoned on the coffee table.

I wander through the hallway. Pause and look at Dorothea's pictures. When she won the Pulitzer, she was happy. But I know from reading her journal that she also fretted whether that collection of poems would be the pinnacle of her career, whether she'd ever write anything else half as good or popular as "Second Kiss." And her fears came true, because the next year Robert Moudowney's wife shot her. Dorothea made the newspapers one more time, but it was for all the wrong reasons.

In the study, Grandmother's dark landscapes seem to suck all the light out of the room. I wonder for about the billionth time why she was so fascinated with storms. Was it her depression? People say she never got over her mother's murder; she was only twelve when it happened. Did she feel the same pressure I do, that Erica does, to live up to her famous mother? Did Granddad contribute to that? By all accounts he was a devoted husband, devastated by her suicide. But he made his career studying her mother's work. That had to be weird sometimes.

What would have happened if Grandmother had made a different choice? If she, like Erica, had run away from Cecil and Granddad instead of walking into the Bay?

These are big, unanswerable questions. But I stand in the middle of the room, staring at the dark clouds and trying to answer them anyhow.

Then Erica screams.

It's not a playful shriek or a frustrated shout. This is a terrifying, bone-chilling sound that makes goose bumps rise on my arms.

I dart to the french doors, looking for the source.

"Grace!" Erica screams. She's standing at the edge of the shore.

There is splashing from out in the water. My sister—my little, strawberry-bubble-gum-chewing, blond-braided sister—is flailing. Choking. Sinking.

I run, kicking off my polka-dot flats.

Her little hand waves in the air. Her head sinks below the water and then pops back up as she kicks and coughs and sputters. She's not a quitter, not the kind to let herself sink. Thank God. My feet thud down the dock, and then I'm in the water with her, cutting through it till I reach her. I snatch Gracie and kick furiously to keep us afloat. She's panicking, making it harder for me to keep hold of her.

"You're okay. Shhh, you're okay. I've got you," I tell her, and she calms enough that I can paddle the few feet back to the dock. Erica leans over and I lift Gracie up to her.

Erica's sobbing, her mascara painting wet, black trails over her cheeks. She drops to her knees, cradling Grace in her arms. "You're okay, baby," she says over and over again. Grace is crying too, and she coughs and throws up water while her mama rubs circles on her back. I haul myself out of the water and kneel next to them.

this is not what drowning looks like

"Are you okay? Did you hit your head?" I ask. Gracie shakes it no.

I reach out and scoop up a sodden soccer ball, which Grace must have been chasing, and heave it back toward the shore.

Erica looks at me. "*Thank you*. I couldn't... I—" She starts sobbing again, holding Grace so tightly that she squirms in protest.

"I'm okay, Mama," she says. "Ivy saved me."

Isobel comes running down through the yard. "Oh my God. What happened? I was up in my room and I heard you scream and—" She takes in Gracie's wet dress, the water dripping from her braids. "Is she okay?"

I nod. "She's fine."

The air is still sultry but Gracie's teeth chatter. "We should get her inside and into dry clothes," Iz suggests. The four of us move together back toward the house, Erica carrying Grace with Iz and me on either side. I pause to grab two towels drying over the porch bannister.

In the kitchen, Erica sets Grace down and Isobel wraps her in one of the towels. Gracie clings to her big sister. "Let's go start a bubble bath," Iz says. "I think Luisa got you strawberry bubbles."

Grace gives her a teary smile. "Will you stay and read me Fancy Nancy?"

Iz nods. "Of course."

"I'm going to make you some hot chocolate, okay?" Erica says. "I'll be up in a minute."

Iz takes Gracie's hand and leads her upstairs. I wrap the other towel around myself, dripping onto Luisa's clean kitchen floor. Erica pours milk into a big mug and puts it in the microwave, then reaches for what I assume will be the hot cocoa mix.

Instead she pulls out a bottle of vodka.

"What are you doing?" I ask.

"Making myself a drink." Erica doesn't meet my eyes, just pours a shot of vodka. Her hand shakes, knocking the bottle against the glass with a sharp clink. "You should probably get into some dry clothes too."

I look at the recycling bin, at the empty wine bottle on top. I pick it up and brandish it at Erica. "Is this why you couldn't save Grace yourself? Because you were already drunk?"

Erica puts her hands on her hips. "I have been drinking, but I'm not drunk."

"Right. Nice distinction. She could have *drowned*!"

"Don't you think I know that? I froze. I haven't been in that water since the day my mother walked in and never came back out," Erica says. "I couldn't do anything to save Mama, and I couldn't do anything to save Grace. It was my worst fucking nightmare, and all I could think was that it was my own damn fault because I should have taught her how to swim."

"You should have," I agree. "Tomorrow, after I get off work at the library, I'll teach her. I taught Abby's little sisters. If we don't get her back in the water, she might get scared of it."

"Like me." Erica takes the shot of vodka and goes to pour another. I grab the bottle out of her hand.

"What do you think you're doing?" She claws at me, leaving a long, red scratch across my forearm.

"If you have one more drink tonight, I swear to God, I will call your ex and tell him what just happened. He deserves to know. And Gracie and Iz deserve a parent who can take care of them."

Erica slumps against the counter. "I'm *trying.*"

"Try harder. Grace could have drowned, and instead of comforting her, you're down here comforting yourself with vodka? What the hell kind of mother are you?" I demand. "They deserve better. Hell, *I* deserve better. But I'm seventeen. I have Granddad and Luisa and Claire and Abby and Connor. Meeting you may not have gone the way I hoped, but I don't *need* you. Iz does though. And Gracie too. She's so little. She really needs her mama."

"I am not this person." Erica raises her mascara-streaked face to me. "I swear. It's being around Dad. Being in this house again. It makes me—"

"No," I interrupt. "I don't want to hear it. Granddad can be pushy and drive me up the wall. Growing up with him is not always a picnic. But he loves me. He loves *you*, despite everything you've done. This town can be claustrophobic, but there are so many good people here who would've helped you if you'd asked. People who probably still would. You are an adult, and you need to stop blaming everything on your parents and me and this town. You need to own your shit."

Erica stares at me, her lips pursed. "Are you done?"

"No." I take a deep breath. "I used to worry that you left because of me. Because you couldn't be my mother. At least with Gracie and Iz you tried. Even last week, when you said I'm someone people leave—that was a really shitty thing to say."

Her gaze falls to the floor, and she fiddles with one of her silver rings. "I know. I'm sorry."

An actual apology. I take the words to heart because I suspect I might never hear them from her again. My voice softens. "I don't hate you. I tried to, but mostly I just feel sad that I'll never know what it's like to have a real mom. Even if someday in the future we can be in the same room without it being awful, it won't be like I grew up with you. And I don't know what you need to do to get better, whether you need a therapist or AA or rehab or what, but—"

"I don't need rehab," Erica snaps. "Stop looking at me like that."

I sigh. "Like what?"

"Like him," she says, and I know she means Granddad. "Like I'm a failure."

I wrap the towel more tightly around me. "Look, I don't care what you do, but you better do something— soon—or Iz and Gracie are going to start looking at you like this too." I put the vodka down on the counter between us. "It's your choice."

CHAPTER

TWENTY

THE HEAT BREAKS IN THE MIDDLE OF THE NIGHT. I WAKE UP TO A
crash of thunder, to lightning bright as day, to a fury of
rain lashing against the roof. I don't know what sixth
sense possesses me—usually I curl up and put my pillow
over my head during thunderstorms—but this time I
crawl out of bed. I walk over to the window under the
eaves and peer down at the side yard.

And I see Erica.

Her spiky blond hair is flattened to her skull, her black
tank top is plastered to her skin, and she's cringing beneath
the onslaught. She's carrying a box in her arms and a bag
over her shoulder.

She's leaving.

I run downstairs in my pajamas but pause in the kitchen when I see the note.

> Dad—
> I'm going away for a while to get myself together. I'll be back this time. I promise.
>
> Grace, Isobel—
> I love you, but your daddy can take better care of you than I can right now.
>
> Ivy—
> I'm sorry. I owe you so many I'm sorrys.

That's all it says. No clue as to where she's going or for how long. She left Isobel's cell phone sitting on top of the note, like a sparkly paperweight.

She's leaving like a thief in the night. Like a coward. *Again.*

I hesitate, but only for a second. Then I run out the back door in my bare feet. Am I too late? Is she already gone?

The cold rain has me shivering in seconds.

Her beat-up Toyota is still in the driveway. She's sitting inside, her face eerie behind the rivulets of rain running down the window. I try the passenger door and it's locked.

City habits run deep, I guess; nobody locks their cars around here. I knock on the window.

For a minute I think she'll drive off and leave me standing here alone in the rain.

Instead she leans over, unlocks the door, and pushes it open.

I slide in. "What the hell are you doing?"

Her face is naked. No makeup. Without it, she looks defenseless. Defeated. "I'm leaving."

"Where are you going?" I ask. "At least tell me where you're going."

She shrugs. "I don't know. Maybe back to New York. I've got some friends there."

I appreciate that she doesn't lie and tell me she's going to rehab when she's not. "Come back inside. No one else has to know about this," I say. "You can put your stuff away. I'll tear up the note. Tomorrow we can figure out a plan, a place for you to go. Somewhere that's not so far away. If you're worried about money, Granddad will take care of it. He just wants—"

"For me to be my best?" Erica's laugh is empty. "I think that ship has sailed, Ivy. No. I can't. I can't look at him and tell him I'm an alcoholic."

She says it easily. Like the words are familiar, not a revelation. My surprise must register on my face because she smiles. "I've been doing AA for years. That's how I met Rick, actually. He kicked me out when he found out I'd started drinking again. I tried to hide it but… God, I hate him for it right now, but he's a good guy. A good dad. He'll take good care of Grace."

"And Iz?" I ask. "Please don't separate them."

"You think I'm a real monster, don't you? Look, I'll sign whatever I need to sign for Rick to have custody. *Temporary* custody," she stresses. "I'm coming back, Ivy."

I bite my lip. "You didn't come back last time. You didn't come back for me."

Without the armor of my anger, I feel so vulnerable. Here it is: the truth. She left me, and I have never forgiven either of us for it.

She reaches over, tentatively, and puts her hand on my arm. "That wasn't your fault."

I've heard that before, but hearing it from *her* breaks something inside me. I start sobbing silently, shaking with the force of it.

And my mother—she sings.

It's just like I remember, the low honey-and-gravel sound of it. The song is beautiful and sad and so, so familiar. It's about going away and coming back home.

"Please come back," I say when my tears have stopped. "Please don't make them feel like this."

"I will, baby." Erica points out the window. The rain still patters against the windshield but less ferociously. The seconds between lightning and thunder have lengthened. "Storm's slowing down. You better go back inside."

"Are you sure this is how you want to do it?" I ask.

She nods. "I know it's shitty, leaving you and Dad to tell the girls… I have no right to ask you this, but—will you try to explain that I'm doing this for them, so they don't hate me?" I nod and she scrubs at her eyes. "Thank you."

I open the door. "You're welcome."

It's the first real conversation I've ever had with my mother. The first time I've felt heard. Loved. *Mothered*.

And now she's leaving. I know she means well; I know she is trying. But I don't know if I will ever see her again.

· · · · ·

I don't go back to sleep. I change clothes and make myself a cup of tea and read at the kitchen table till the sun is up. Then I go upstairs to wake Granddad, the note and Isobel's cell phone clutched in my hand. He comes out of his bedroom as I raise my hand to knock.

We haven't spoken much since I left Java Jim's. When he came home and found out how Gracie almost drowned, he hugged me tight and thanked God that I'd gotten there in time. Erica stood nearby with a sour look on her face. Like every time he said something nice to me, it took something away from her.

We all sat around the table and had ice cream. It was the first time—and now maybe the last—that we were together as a family without a fight. Gracie was back to her chipper self quicker than the rest of us. I couldn't stop worrying about what might have happened if I hadn't left the open mic night early. Would Erica have gotten past her fear of the water and saved Gracie, or would I have lost my little sister? Erica was quiet the rest of the evening, hovering over Grace, maybe wondering the same thing.

I hand Granddad the note. He reads it and cusses, running a hand over his beard. "Not again."

"I saw her before she left. She said she'll be back this time," I offer.

"Are you all right?" Granddad's eyes search my face like he's looking for clues. Waiting for me to break, maybe. But I am learning I'm an awful lot more resilient than he or I or anyone else has been giving me credit for.

"I am, actually," I say. And I mean it. I'm sad—really sad—but I'm okay.

"Will you stay home this morning and help me look after the girls? She might do a poor job of it sometimes, but Erica's the only mother they've ever known, and her walking out like this…"

We're still talking in hushed voices. A few yards away, the girls are sleeping behind their closed door. "Of course.

I'll call the library and let them know there's a family emergency. I'm sure they'll understand."

"I think that's best," Granddad agrees. "But maybe say you're not feeling well. No need for people to start asking questions."

Part of me wants to lash out at him the same way I did Erica. Denounce him for his damned pride, for all the ways he's contributed to this mess. But his shoulders are slumped and his blue eyes are watery and bleary pre-coffee. This is a lot for anyone to deal with once, let alone twice.

I'm not the only one who's had to endure the whispers and poor-dearing over the years. How much shame must he have felt when Erica ran away the first time and left me behind? Whatever was or wasn't his fault, she was the daughter he raised, and every arrow that people in this town slung in her direction must have felt like it went through him first.

"No one needs to know the details, but it seems kind of pointless to lie," I say. "People will find out that Erica's gone."

"Ivy, I really don't need everyone in town speculating about what's wrong with my daughter, whether she went to rehab, whether she's in a psychiatric hospital, whether it's like mother, like daughter."

For a minute I think he means me. That *I'm* bound to inherit Erica's problems. Then I realize that he means Erica and Grandmother.

"What am I supposed to say? I don't even know where she went," he says.

"I think we have to trust that she's going to get better so she can come back for Gracie and Iz." It sounds ludicrous, even to me, but what other choice do we have? "She knew she was going to lose them anyway. After what happened yesterday, one of us was going to call her ex."

"I tried to get her help before. Therapy. Inpatient stays for her eating disorder. As soon as she turned eighteen, she refused to go back. I guess Grace falling in the water yesterday was a wake-up call," Granddad muses. "But her leaving again? People will talk."

"They will." I take a deep breath, already dreading all the questions.

The door across the hall creaks open. It's Iz, her blond hair in wild curls around her face. She steps out into the hallway and shuts the door behind her. "What's going on? I can hear you two whispering." She sees her phone in Granddad's hand. "Did Mama give you that?"

Granddad nods. "Isobel, let's go downstairs."

Iz scrunches up her face. "Now? It's barely morning."

"I think it would be good for us to talk before Grace wakes up," Granddad says, herding us toward the stairs.

Iz darts a glance over her shoulder at me, her brown eyes enormous. "What happened? Is Mama... Is she dead?"

My heart aches that that was her first thought.

"No. But she's gone away for a while," Granddad says.

"What do you mean, gone?" Iz asks.

We file into the kitchen and Granddad hands her the note. She reads it and slumps into a chair.

"Where did she go? When is she coming back?" Iz asks.

Granddad and I exchange looks. "We don't know."

"What if she *doesn't* come back? What if she leaves us here forever, like she did with you?" Iz turns to me, her voice rising. "What if Dad doesn't want me either? What will happen to me? Where will I live?"

Granddad sits down next to her. Puts a hand on her shoulder. His hands are big and wrinkled, his knuckles swollen from arthritis. "You will always have a home here, Isobel. We're your family."

"I want to talk to her. I want to know where she is. When she's coming back." Isobel dials her mother's number and puts the phone to her ear. Her leg jiggles frantically. "It goes right to voice mail. She probably sees that it's me. She probably sees that it's me and she isn't answering her fucking phone! What kind of mama—?" Her voice breaks.

"We're here, Iz. You aren't alone," I promise her.

"I'm going to call Rick," Granddad says. "Can you give me his number, Isobel? You can talk to him after I've had a chance to explain what's happened."

"Here, use my phone." Iz hands it back to him. "He's under 'Dad.'"

Gracie and Iz are going away. That's all I can think. If Rick is half the man his daughters think he is, he'll cancel everything and be here in a few hours to take them home.

I only had ten days with them.

It's not fair. We're sisters. We should get to grow up together.

I fight against another surge of anger at Erica. I was supposed to have this summer with them, at least.

"Ivy, after you call in sick at the library, will you call down to the Sutton and tell Saundra that Isobel won't be able to make it?" Granddad asks.

"Tell her I'm not coming back," Iz says.

"Let's wait and see what your father has to say. He might not be able to come get you right away."

Isobel glares. "Even if I'm stuck here, I'm not going back to that stupid theater camp."

"Isobel, honey, let's wait until we have more information. I already paid for the whole month," Granddad says.

Iz gives him a look that is pure Erica. "Then that's your own fault for wasting your money. I told you I didn't want to go. You didn't listen to me. Nobody ever listens to me except Dad."

Granddad frowns. "I know you're upset with your mother right now, and I understand that, but you need to speak to me with respect."

"There's room to be upset with both of you." Iz

straightens the leg of her purple-plaid pajama pants, and I fall a little more in love with my new sister. Sure, she can be a brat, but she's brave enough to say what she thinks, to tell the truth, and in this family, that's worth a hell of a lot.

"She's right," I say, and they both turn to stare at me. "Well, she is. She told you no and you didn't listen. This is going to be hard enough, and if you don't let us handle it the way we need to—within reason, I mean— it's going to be harder. Iz shouldn't have to go to theater camp. And I'm not going to lie to people about what happened. You can play it off like Erica was always planning a short visit, but I'm not going to spin some pretty lie. I don't think it's okay for you to ask me to, any more than it was okay for Erica to ask me to lie about being their sister."

I think Granddad will argue with me, but he doesn't. "You're right," he says. "I'm sorry. You tell people whatever you want."

He takes Isobel's phone and goes to his study to call Rick. I sit at the table with Iz while she stares at Erica's note, trying to make sense of it.

"You bitched her out yesterday, didn't you?" Isobel asks. She looks so young now, without her makeup, with her tousled-every-which-way hair and pajamas.

"I told her you and Gracie deserve a better mother."

I say the words slowly, carefully. Isobel is searching for someone to blame, and it would be easy for her to pin Erica's leaving on me.

Iz smiles sadly. "I always thought a bad mother was better than none at all."

"I don't know." I have given this a lot of thought over the last week. "It was hard sometimes. Luisa took me bra shopping and to the gynecologist for the first time, and Claire gave me the sex talk before anybody else." That earns a smile from Iz. "Mother's Days were the worst. I was so jealous of my friends. I used to give Luisa presents, but it wasn't the same. When I was little, like Gracie's age, I used to wish Erica would come back. I wished on shooting stars and four-leaf clovers and pennies in fountains. And then she came back and she—"

"She pretended she wasn't even your mama." Isobel winces.

"Yep. And it really sucked. But I got through it, more or less. And you will too."

"How?" Iz asks. "What if Mama's right and Dad doesn't want me? What if Gracie goes home today and I have to stay here by myself and go to that stupid theater camp?"

"You won't be by yourself. You'll have me. And you don't have to go back to theater camp." My voice is firm. "I'll talk to Granddad for you if you want. You've inspired me, Iz. I want to be more like you."

Iz looks down at the silver nail polish peeling off her bitten-down fingernails. "Like *me*?"

I nod. "You tell the truth even when it's hard. You tell people what you want. I'm going to start doing that more too and make Granddad listen. He's not in the habit of it, so it might be hard at first. I'm going to start off by telling him about Connor."

"He already knows about that. I kind of told him this weekend. I didn't know it was a secret." Iz grins, twirling a curl around her finger.

Wait, Granddad knew and he still left Connor and me alone yesterday morning? With no one but Erica in the house, and no lecture? Maybe he does trust me. "Oh. Well, thanks. When do I get to see a picture of Kyle?"

Iz tosses her hair over her shoulder. "Never. I broke up with him yesterday. He was such a douche bag. All he wanted to do was have sexy video chats, and he got all mad when I wouldn't take my shirt off or talk dirty. It was gross."

"Good for you. You deserve better."

"I think I do." She blushes. "Thanks."

Quiet stretches out between us, but for the first time it's a comfortable quiet. Then:

"Ivy?" Iz says, her voice soft.

"Yeah?"

"I'm sorry I was a bitch before. I didn't ever think... I

was so mad at you for lying that I didn't think about how much this sucked for you too," she confesses.

"You don't ever have to apologize for your feelings," I tell her. "I would have been mad too if I were you."

"But I didn't ever tell you I'm glad you're my sister," she says. "And I am."

I look at her—my brave-as-hell little sister—and grin. "I am too."

. . . . .

It takes a while to get everything settled. Gracie wakes up to the news that her mama is gone, but we all assure her—hopefully, truthfully—that Erica's gone away to get better and will be back soon. That she's doing it because she loves Gracie and Iz and wants to be a better mama.

Rick arrives midafternoon. There is never any question of whether he'll take Isobel too. "She's my daughter in every way that counts," he says. He's tall and lanky and kind. He helps the girls finish packing and promises to bring them back the following weekend with a truck to get the rest of their things and to visit us. He apologizes profusely for Erica. If he's mad that we kept quiet about how bad things were, he doesn't say so in front of the girls.

Luisa bakes chocolate-chip cookies for them to take home. Gracie and Iz help, bickering over who gets to lick the batter from the spoon. Luisa watches them and wraps an arm around my waist. I lean into her, comforting myself with her steady presence.

Alex even pops in at one point. "Hey, I heard you two were going back to DC," he says. "I wanted to say bye."

"You just want our cookies!" Gracie accuses him, while Iz blushes. Unless I am mistaken, I think somebody's got a crush.

Alex grins and grabs a cookie from the counter. "That too." He dances around the kitchen like a goofball and the girls giggle. He looks over and meets my eyes. "You have a minute?"

I nod and slip out of the kitchen into the backyard. He stands next to me on the patio, hands shoved in the pockets of his cargo shorts. I am not sure what to expect, given the last thing I said to him was to go to hell, but...

"You okay?" he asks.

"I'm really going to miss them," I admit.

"They're pretty cute."

"I think Iz thinks *you're* pretty cute," I joke without thinking.

"What? Shut up," he says, giving me a playful push. Then his shoulders stiffen and he shoves his hands back into his pockets. "I've gotta get to work. But I wanted to check on you."

"Thanks," I say. "I appreciate that."

It feels weird and stilted, and I'm not sure if our friend-ship will ever be the same. But he's here. He asked if I was okay. That means something.

Later, Granddad and I stand with Gracie and Iz around Rick's black SUV to say our good-byes. The afternoon sun beats down on the crown of my head and the pavement is hot beneath my feet. It reminds me of the afternoon the girls showed up in my life. Now they're leaving, and it feels like the house will be too quiet without them.

Gracie wraps her arms around my waist and hugs me tight. "Thank you for saving me." She looks up at her dad. "Did Granddad tell you what happened, Daddy? I fell in the water and almost drowned, but Ivy jumped in and saved me. She's like a superhero!"

"She is a hero," Rick agrees, mouthing *thank you* at me over her shoulder.

"I'm going to miss you," Gracie says fiercely.

"Me too. But we can video-chat."

"And you can come visit us in DC whenever you want. You're family," Rick says, and I think my heart grows three sizes. Even Isobel gives me a quick, awkward hug.

As they drive down the lane, Granddad and I are both a little sniffly. He clears his throat. "Allergies."

Liar. He doesn't have any allergies. I put my arm around his waist, leaning into his shoulder. "You've still got me."

Granddad smiles down at me. "Thank God for that. You

were a huge help with the girls. I know you've only had a week or so, but you're a good big sister. I'm proud of you."

I start sniffling again. "Really?"

"Absolutely. You know, after you left Java Jim's last night, I had a talk with Connor."

"Really? Um, what did you talk about?" I bite my lip.

"He thought that you ran out because I was putting undue pressure on you. That maybe you don't understand how proud I am of you." Granddad looks down at me. "Maybe I don't say it often enough, but you are the light of my life, Ivy. If I push you too hard sometimes, it's only because you're so bright, so curious, and I want you to know that you can do or be whatever you want."

"But I can't do and be *everything*," I say. "Sometimes I'm not sure I can do *anything*. I don't have a gift like Dorothea or Grandmother or Erica. I'm so—mediocre."

"Mediocre?" Granddad roars. "Bullshit. No granddaughter of mine is mediocre."

I laugh through my tears. "Language, Granddad."

"You are a remarkably capable girl, Ivy. Women twice your age—hell, women *my* age—would have fallen apart with everything you've been through these last two weeks. And instead you kept this family together. You called people out on things when they needed it, myself included. And you seem to have found yourself a good young man."

I blush. "You kind of found him for me."

My phone chimes with a text. "Speak of the devil," I say.

Are you okay? Connor asks.

We've been texting all day. He didn't tell me that he talked to Granddad, but I think that's one secret I can forgive.

Not yet, I text back. **But I will be.**

And I stand there in the driveway with Granddad, and I think it might be true.

ACKNOWLEDGMENTS

Every book is a journey, but this book has changed an awful lot since the first pages I scribbled back in fall 2013, inspired by the poems of Edna St. Vincent Millay and by April Genevieve Tucholke's *Between the Devil and the Deep Blue Sea*. I set out to write my own book about family ghosts and poetry and the ocean, and while there's no longer a ghost in *Wild Swans*, this draft couldn't have existed without that one. Thank you to Sara Sargent for her tremendously helpful thoughts on that early draft.

Thank you to my agent, Jim McCarthy, who told me that it was more than okay to try something new and urged me to follow my heart on this book. Thank you to Annette Pollert-Morgan for an edit letter full of inspiring character-driven questions; to Elizabeth Boyer and Diane Dannenfeldt for their copyedits; to Brittany Vibbert for a gorgeous cover design that is everything I dreamed of; to Jillian Rahn for the lovely interior design; to Alex Yeadon for connecting my book with readers; and to everyone else at Sourcebooks who has championed *Wild Swans*.

Thank you to the wonderful staff at One More Page and Politics and Prose bookstores for being so supportive; to the Highlights Foundation for their magical Unworkshops; and to the staff at Peregrine for keeping me supplied with iced black tea while I wrote and edited this book.

Thank you to Tiffany for being an amazing cheerleader and friend; to Lauren for brainstorming walks at Highlights; to Lindsay for encouraging line edits; and to Anna-Marie for insightful notes on Ella's scenes. To Caroline and Robin for five-plus years of flailmails. To Miranda for answering my newbie "how do I write contemporary" questions. To Andrea, Marie, and Beth for always inspiring me to dream a little bigger.

Connor's heartbreak over his grams was inspired by the slow decline of my Papaw to Alzheimer's and by my bookish Memaw, who would be thrilled to pieces that I am now a librarian and an author. I miss them both more than I can convey.

Special thanks to my mom, who is much more of a

Luisa (baking delicious cookies, growing beautiful flowers, and making me laugh) than an Erica. Thank you to all my wonderfully supportive family and friends, especially to my BFFs Jenn and Jill, who are just as smart and funny and loyal as Claire and Abby. I couldn't let Ivy have any less.

Most especially, thank you to my husband, who has thoroughly convinced me that bookish boys with tattoos are the best.

ABOUT THE AUTHOR

Jessica Spotswood is the author of the Cahill Witch Chronicles (*Born Wicked, Star Cursed,* and *Sisters' Fate*) and the editor of the feminist historical anthology *A Tyranny of Petticoats.* She grew up in a tiny, one-stoplight town in Pennsylvania, where she could be found swimming, playing clarinet, memorizing lines for the school play, or—most often—with her nose in a book. Now she lives in Washington, DC, where she can be found working as a children's library associate for the DC Public Library, seeing theater with her playwright husband, or—most often—with her nose in a book. Some things never change.